THE VOICE OF EVIL

"Adrienne! Adrienne!" The voice was low, commanding, deep, near.

The girl awakened from her stupor, stirred on the hard ground, and drew her wet cloak about her with a deep, weary shudder. The voice—it had seemed so close! She gazed about her into the darkness, but saw no one.

"Adrienne! Adrienne! Adrienne! Answer me!"

"I am—here—" she muttered. She felt ill, feverish, dazed. She spoke into the darkness, and in the darkness came the answer.

"Speak again, Adrienne! Speak again, I command you!"

"Here—here—I am here," she said, weakly. She sank down again on the ground. She wanted to sleep, to sleep, and not to waken. The horrors she had seen and experienced pressed too close. Life was not welcome. . . .

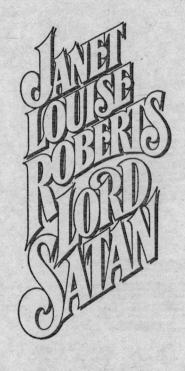

JANET LOUISE ROBERTS

LORD SATAN

PUBLISHED BY POCKET BOOKS NEW YORK

POCKET BOOKS, a Simon & Schuster division of
GULF & WESTERN CORPORATION
1230 Avenue of the Americas, New York, N.Y. 10020

ISBN: 0-671-81306-4

First Pocket Books printing September, 1979

10 9 8 7 6 5 4 3 2 1

Trademarks registered in the United States and other countries.

Printed in the U.S.A.

CHAPTER 1

Adrienne Caudill was informed on reaching the White Stag Inn that the coach was only an hour and a quarter late, having made excellent time. Fatigued, her bonnet set sideways on her blonde curls, she could only nod and try to smile. She was so weary she wished only to stretch her limbs and wash her face.

Rain had been pouring down for the past two hours, as the coach had lumbered its way along the Cornish moors, past flat lands and glimpses of small neat farms. Adrienne had peered out again and again, curious at this look at a new land. She had lived near the sea, on the South Coast, all her seventeen years.

She could not keep the unwelcome reflection from herself that she did much prefer the sea, the blue, the green, the wild, the lovely sea, in all its moods. But her life was to be changed now, changed forever, and there was not much she could do about it. All she could do was accept the changes, and hope for the best.

She tried to think of an appropriate poem to suit the mood, yet even this failed her. Her father had quoted poetry by the hour, in addition to making up his own, and Adrienne had formed the habit of writing small shy verses of her own. But the events of the past months had been so big, so appalling, that she could not find refuge even in writing poetry.

Her dear father was dead. The pillar of her life, the stalwart strength which had upheld her always, especially the times since her mother had died when she was ten, he was now gone. Injured at sea, a rope line catching and flinging him against an iron post, lying helplessly for months, finally dying with her mother's name on his lips. Tears began to form again in her large blue eyes. She looked at rain-blurred landscape through thick lashes filled with salt tears. This would never do, she thought.

She was fortunate in having one relative left in the

5

world, and he a wealthy man, Lord of Castle Caudill. He had written a kindly letter to her, when she had informed him of her father's death. She was to come with her maid to this White Stag Inn, and he would meet her and convey her to his home. He would have a care for her, as she had been related to his late beloved mother, he had said.

She had clung to the words, during the times of packing, selling the small cottage by the sea, and her father's share in the boat. She had clung to the lines of his letters, the large upright bold hand in the black ink, reading them again and again for comfort. He would have a care for her, a care for her—

She left the coach at the White Stag Inn. A careless landlord in a dirty smock greeted her curtly, turning up his nose, she thought, at the intelligence that she had no maid with her. He had conveyed her to the inn parlor, and told her curtly there was no man there to meet her.

"But we are—quite late," she whispered timidly, gazing up at him anxiously. "Surely—no one has come—and gone again?"

"No one has come at all, miss, not for you," he said roughly, giving a glance at her ancient grey cloak, her grey bonnet, the tumbled blonde curls and mended grey gloves. "I'm expecting a grand gentleman, and he has the good parlor. You're not to go in there, miss! Mind, now."

"Oh, yes, sir, I shan't go in there," she said hastily. They passed the good parlor, and she had a glimpse of china and crystal set grandly on a white lace cloth, flowers in a vase, and oh—the smell of roast beef, and greens, and pastries, and a dozen wine bottles were set out on side tables. She was aware of an immense hunger.

Might she ask for tea and bread? She opened her lips to request them, she had a little money with her to pay. But the landlord left her at the door of the inn parlor, and raced out again to the courtyard.

Discouraged, she went into the dark parlor, and removed her cloak and bonnet. She saw herself in a dingy mirror, and exclaimed. "Oh, dear, how dreadful, I look a fright!" She tried to smooth down the ruffled blonde curls, but nothing restored color to the pale weary face or brightened the tired blue eyes. She sat down limply on the horsehide sofa, and tried to be grateful that it was not swaying and lurching like the coach seat.

She searched in the large faded flowery carpetbag for the beloved much-read letter, and read it slowly again.

She had not mistaken the day. The bold handwriting said the day, the time the coach would arrive, the place, all very clearly.

He would come, he must come, she thought. She drooped against the hard sofa, and wished she might sleep. It was growing late in the day, the sky had faded to a misty darker grey, the rain was clearing, but it was growing colder. Did they have a long way yet to go?

October, 1815. And she was but seventeen, she mused, staring unseeingly at the lines of the comforting letter. Where would she be when she was eighteen—and nineteen? Would he obtain a post for her, as a governess, perhaps? What would he do with her? She sighed, deeply, then sat up straight, and tried to brace her courage.

Suddenly she was aware of a powerful strong masculine voice. And it was saying words—oh, such words! She had heard some of them a few times, from some of the rougher fishermen who worked with her father. On impulse, she jumped up from the sofa, and went to the door of the parlor, but she heard little. The girl went on down the hall, to the courtyard door of the inn—and stared, wide-eyed at the sight before her.

The coach from which she had stepped down was still in the courtyard, empty. The horses were being changed. Near the coach was a smart carriage, with golden trim and dark red paint, with a crest on the door. But she had no eyes for this now.

The tall dark-haired man commanded all her attention, and indeed the attention of the entire force of the inn. The landlord was cringing before him, at the cold hard voice, at the cursing which was being flung at him.

"You are a damned bastard, you ought to be whipped! I gave you explicit instructions! You were to have the lady wait in comfort, you were to give her every care—"

"But she—did not come—" the landlord wailed.

The man lifted his hands, in smart black gloves, and the landlord cringed as though expecting to be struck. The man cursed him again, deliberately, his dark green eyes flashing like fiery coals.

A stableboy near Adrienne whispered as though to himself, "Cor! If I could talk like that swell!"

"Who is the man?" asked Adrienne softly.

The stableboy glanced up at her, his dark eyes wide. "Lor', he's Lord Satan, he is!"

She caught her breath sharply. Lord Satan! Lord Satan!

She thought of John Milton's marvelous poem, "Paradise Lost," and the lines her father had quoted in his sonorous voice, about Lucifer, who had fallen from the sky, and become Satan.

> ". . . he above the rest
> In shape and gesture proudly eminent
> Stood like a Tower; his form had yet not lost
> All her original brightness, nor appeared
> Less than Arch Angel ruined, and the excess
> Of Glory obscured—"

She murmured a phrase to herself, "Arch Angel—ruined—" and looked fascinated at the man. He was like Lucifer himself, she thought, proud, haughty, his cheek scarred in a strange line from left eye to left side of the mouth in an irregular pattern. As he cursed the landlord afresh, she stared at him, wide-eyed, and listened to the melodic flow of the terrible words, the wild grand inflection of his voice. She watched the proud passionate face, the imperious toss of the black head.

Then abruptly, he turned, and saw her staring at him. His voice stopped abruptly. He stared at her in turn. The green eyes were flashing, the gaze seemed to sear her. She could not move, nor take her look from his.

As he stared, his face changed. It seemed to light from a radiance within, and she thought, "Like Lucifer—before the fall!" She gazed, bewildered, as he strode toward her. As he came, in a lithe graceful walk, he stripped off his thick black gloves, and she saw his white hands, large, graceful, smooth. One was held out to her.

He came close. His hand was still out, imperiously. She put her own small one in it, slowly, she could not deny him. He smiled down at her, glancing over her tumbled blonde hair, the wide blue eyes, the pale weary face, the small rounded body in the shabby grey dress.

He said, "Adrienne," and she thought her name had never sounded so beautiful. "Adrienne. You came."

"Yes, sir," she said softly.

"Come," he said, and turned her shoulders gently so that she went before him into the inn. He paused at the door of the good parlor, and conducted her inside. She turned toward him, opened her mouth to explain that it was for some special grand gentleman—then she understood.

He was the grand gentleman. And he must be her cousin.

"Little Adrienne," he said again, in a gentle melodic persuasive voice. "How weary you must be, and to be greeted like this! Come, sit down. You shall have a small glass of wine, just your size, and then a good dinner, before we continue to the castle. Where is your maid?" He glanced about, as though expecting a respectable woman to materialize.

"Oh, sir, I am sorry, I have no maid. It was necessary for me to come alone." She gazed up at him trustfully as he set a glass in her hand. The wine was red, bubbly, stronger than any she had had. But he seemed to know just what he was doing.

"You came alone? So you have courage as well as beauty, little cousin! Oh, forgive me. I have not introduced myself, I felt as though we knew each other already!" And he smiled down at her with great charm. "I am Vincent Stanton, your cousin."

"Yes, sir," she said, and thought of his titles, among them, Lord Devereux, Lord of Castle Caudill, Viscount of something else, and on and on.

"You must call me Vincent, and I shall call you Adrienne," he said, comfortably, and seated himself in the plump chair beside her. A maid came in to cut the meat and place large slices on beautiful china plates. He raised his glass to her lips. She still hesitated. "Drink it, little one. It will put some color in your cheeks, and strengthen you for the long journey I fear is still before you. It is another five hours to your future home."

She could not repress a sigh, but lifted the glass obediently. It tasted strong, fiery, yet good. She sipped it cautiously, and he watched her with a little smile.

"You are like a little blonde angel," he said musingly. "You look like you should be dusted and replaced on the shelf, to be an ornament and a joy to all in the castle." Mischievously he reached out and tugged one of her blonde curls.

She stiffened, and said earnestly, "Oh, sir, I'm used to hard work. Really, sir! I shall earn my keep, I assure you! I have kept the house, and cleaned, and am counted a fairly good cook. I have learned my sums and can read and write—"

His teasing smile altered, he kept gazing at her as though he would study her and know her through and

9

through. He took her free hand, and studied it, looked at the redness and roughness of it lying in his large smooth white hand.

"So—you have worked hard, little one? Yes, I see that. Well, you shall have a rest at the castle, your new home, I assure you. One so pretty and dainty should never have to work. But—all that later. Come, let us eat, and be on our way." He rose, and drew her over to the table, where the maid waited anxiously to see if he would approve of her serving. His glance flicked over the table, he directed her in two matters, which she corrected at once.

Then he drew out a chair for Adrienne, and seated her as though she were a grand lady. He sat across from her, and served her plate and teased her into eating more than she had wanted.

There were rich slices of roast beef, and thick gravy, and potatoes, and greens, and some fruit tart. And with it the hearty tea she craved. She drank two china cups of the fine tea, and gently refused more wine.

"Indeed, sir, the wine I have had has made my head so queerish," she said, earnestly. "I fear I am not accustomed to it."

"It is not an occasion for apology," he said, and changed the conversation. She was aware that he watched her closely, though his glance flicked away when it seemed to embarrass her. She wondered if she ate with the correct forks, or if she looked too country and dowdy for him. He had been flattering to her, but perhaps it was just to set her at ease. He had the air of a great gentleman, she thought, and surely the really great gentleman had the gift of being gracious to even the most lowly of their relatives.

Finally they finished. He escorted her out to his grand coach with a flourish. She found her small trunk and her faded carpetbag had been placed inside by someone. The landlord smirked and groveled before her as he did before the lord, who dismissed him curtly and glared at him.

In the coach, the lord said, "I do not endure fools gladly," and he sounded quite enraged, his green eyes blazing again. "He did not follow my orders. You were to be given every comfort and attention on your arrival. I warned him of my late arrival."

He gave the signal to his groom, who sprang up on

the box. Soon the coach was rolling so smoothly down the highway that she gave a sigh of relief. It was not at all like the lurching and swaying of the public coach, she thought. This was so—luxurious, so easy.

"I expect," she said, after the little pause, "that the landlord did not expect me to be—the—the lady you expected. That is why he was so—so unwelcoming."

"You would find excuses for—the devil himself," said her cousin musingly. He smiled down at her quickly, his green eyes mischievous. "Would you not, cousin?"

"I do not know, sir," she said, startled, thinking of the way the stableboy had spoken of him. "Lord Satan!"

"You are weary, lean back and rest. Sleep if you can. It is a long journey yet before we arrive home." He settled himself back in the coach, against the comfortable velvet puffs, and seemed to take his own advice, closing his disturbing eyes.

She finally stirred herself and settled back against the cushions. He had put a warm rug about her, and she felt so very good, with the fine dinner and wine inside her, and the thick fur rug over her, and the gentleness with which he had treated her.

Her eyes were heavy. She closed them, her thick lashes resting on her cheeks. She would not sleep—but she would—rest—for a little time—rest her eyes—

The rain had started again, and the hard clatter of it on the roof made her glad she was inside the coach, and so very warm—and cared for— Her head dropped, she jerked it upright, it drooped again—found a resting place, and with a sigh she gave herself up to sleep.

She was only vaguely aware of the horses being pulled up, of shouting and a smooth voice telling someone to be quiet. She stirred and sat up slowly, looking about.

"Oh—shall we—stop—for a time?" she asked sleepily.

"We are home, little cousin. So you are finally awake?" There was amusement and tenderness in his tone. His arms were only slowly falling from around her.

She had slept, she was aware, against his chest! That was the warm strong refuge her head had found, and the hard beat, which in her dreams she had thought was the sea, had been the even strong beat of his heart under her ear. She lifted her hand to her bonnet, flushed to find it had been removed and was lying near the floor of the coach, on the fur rug.

The coach had pulled up at the foot of a long steep

11

flight of stairs. She peered out past his broad shoulders, and thought she would never make it. Up, up the long stone steps loomed the towers of a huge stone castle, immense, grim, forbidding. "Oh—it is so huge—so very big," she whispered, aghast.

"You shall be comfortable here, little one," he reassured her quickly. "Come—" He had stepped out, and reached in the coach to help her. She stumbled getting out, she was still half-asleep. Before she knew it, he had swung her up in his powerful arms, and was carrying her easily up the long flight of stairs.

She blinked up at him. "I can walk, sir!"

He smiled down at her. "I doubt that, my little angel. You are still asleep. Trust me," he said, gently. "I will not let you fall."

He carried her into a huge entrance hall, where torches lit a grim stone floor, huge walls, iron and steel weapons on the mammoth ceiling and walls, thick red hangings decorated with battle flags.

He set her down gently in the entrance room beyond, where a neat woman waited her, wearing a black satin gown.

"Adrienne, this is Mrs. Griffith, my housekeeper. Mrs. Griffith, you will have every care of my little cousin, Miss Adrienne Caudill!"

The housekeeper was staring at her, forgetting to speak. Adrienne thought she must look indeed a fright, or was it that the older woman was shocked at the lord carrying her in that fashion?

She smiled timidly, finally held out her hand shyly. It was received warmly in a large almost masculine grip. "Welcome to Castle Caudill, my—Miss Caudill," said the woman slowly.

"She is very weary. You shall take her up to her rooms, tuck her into bed, and bring her some hot tea. Will that suit you, Adrienne?" said the man standing behind her. She could feel the heat of his body close to hers, like some protecting guardian, she thought vaguely.

"Oh, yes, sir, I regret I am so very tired," she said, and added, "Tomorrow I shall learn my duties, and I shall try very hard to please you!"

Unexpectedly, he chuckled. He touched her cheek with a careless finger. "You please me already, little cousin. Come, I'll show you your rooms, and you shall tell me if you like them!"

The housekeeper went before them, her black satin skirts swishing up the broad stone staircase. The center of the stairs was covered with a dark red carpet, and at the landing were fine marble statues such as Adrienne had seen in books of Greece.

Then at the top of the stairs, just past the landing, he paused, and made her stop by touching her with his hand at her elbow. "Look, Adrienne. Do you know who this is?"

He was pointing up at a painting. She blinked, and started. "Oh—it looks like—oh—"

The woman in the large painting was blonde, and small, and pretty, her face so sweet and gentle that she seemed to welcome Adrienne with her smile. The long hair hung in blonde curls, the eyes were as green as Vincent Stanton's flashing green eyes. But the face, the form, were like those of Adrienne and of her own lost mother.

"She looks—like my mother—and me," whispered Adrienne.

He smiled down at her. "Yes, I lost my mother some years ago, little one. When I saw you today, I thought for a moment that she had returned to me. I—loved her dearly. You are doubly welcome here, dear Adrienne. For yourself—and for your resemblance to my own lost one."

He tucked her hand in his arm and they on down to the door where the housekeeper waited for them. Adrienne felt overwhelmed. Vincent's hard face had softened marvelously as he had spoken of his mother. He had loved her, as much as she had loved her own mother. And she resembled his mother.

She had no time to puzzle about this, or realize its implications. Vincent ushered her into a huge room. She gasped, her eyes growing so wide she thought they must fill her face.

The large room was a living room, with beautiful cream-colored drapes, flowered sofas and chairs, little puffy stools for footrests, plump cushions and flowers everywhere on small marble-topped carved-wood tables. The rug was a precious French one, a large oval in cream and rose and blue. Vincent trod on it as though not even seeing it, leading her beyond the room to the bedroom.

"I hope you will be comfortable here, little one," he said, and drew her into the bedroom. It was almost as

13

large as the living room. It was dominated by an immense carved wood bed of rich cherry color, topped by an immense canopy of cream-silk, puffed with thick spread of matching cream satin. Everywhere were vases of flowers, roses, and cream and blue flowers of unknown varieties which gave forth a subtle scent.

Vincent flicked her cheek carelessly, and departed before she could thank him. She was overwhelmed, speechless, so weary that tears filled her eyes as the housekeeper helped her undress and put her into the immense bed.

CHAPTER 2

When Adrienne woke the next morning, it was to sunshine streaming in the long wide windows and flowing like beaten gold over the cream of her satin sheets and blankets. She felt so warm, so comfortable, that she curled like a kitten and yawned and stretched happily for a time before she quite remembered where she was.

She lay back on the plump pillows, gazing about her with awe. The ceiling which she could see beyond the cream canopy was decorated with imps and cupids, with Venus-figures and gods and goddesses she could not name. All was cream and gold with carved white figures in the corners near the ceilings. Her gaze wandered about, to the velvet sofa, so small and pretty, in a corner, the velvet of a pretty cream, the cushions of rose and blue. There was a plump small armchair, just her size, she thought, of more cream velvet.

"Ohh," she whispered. "I cannot—believe—this!"

That such luxury could exist in the world, she had never believed. That it should fall to her lot to be ensconced in the midst of it—she could not believe! Was she still dreaming? She pinched herself vigorously, said, "Ouch!" and began to believe it.

A voice said, "Is the little lady awake?" and a middle-aged lady peeped around the corner of the door, and smiled to see her sitting up, small in the immensity of the gigantic bed. "Yes, you are, and such a dear! I am Rosa, Miss Adrienne. I brought you tea last night, but you were just about asleep."

"Oh, yes, you are Rosa." Adrienne smiled at her happily. The maid came in, and deposited an armload of clothing on a low chest near the bed.

"You shall have a lovely hot bath, miss, and then my lord sent a selection of clothing for you. They were the late lady's, miss, my lord's mother. He thought the blue dresses would suit you best, but if you choose the rose he will be pleased, or the cream is lovely with your coloring." The maid held up dresses in turn, gazing critically at them.

"Oh—they are t—too grand for me!" Adrienne gasped.

"They are sadly out of fashion. But my lady had excellent taste. My lord thought you might wear some of them until he can order more from London." Briskly, the maid drew a bath in the large pink and cream bathroom, helped Adrienne bathe, poured oil on her soft skin, rubbed her down, powdered her, perfumed her, then dressed her in exquisite lace and silk underclothing.

"Where—where is my—own clothing?" quavered Adrienne, touching the frilly wisps of nothing.

"My lord said they were not to be unpacked. My lord said you should have prettier clothes, miss. Now, will you wear a blue dress, or a rose, or a cream?"

Adrienne's head was in a whirl. She reached out silently for the nearest dress, which was a blue silk, with a soft frill of white about the neck. The maid put it on her, and exclaimed in satisfaction as Adrienne sat at the dressing table to have her blonde hair brushed out.

"Yes, that is lovely. The white standing up about your little neck—and the blue is the color of your eyes. My lord will be pleased!"

"Is—is my lady—about?" asked Adrienne timidly.

"My lady? She has been dead these sixteen years, miss!"

"I meant—my lady—that is, cousin Vincent's wife."

The maid stared down at her. "My lord has never taken a wife," she said.

"Oh," said Adrienne, and was aware of a sudden guilty rush of pleasure. So he was not married. The maid was smiling a bit, knowingly, and Adrienne blushed more deeply.

It was almost noon. The maid conducted her down

the broad staircase she had gone up in such a daze the night before. Rosa took her past one room and another, and finally turned in at a lovely drawing room.

"My lord will join you here, and take you in to luncheon, miss," she said, and departed.

Adrienne wandered about the beautiful room. She was too excited to sit still. There were art objects scattered about the small carved wood tables, and she picked up one curiously. It was a pale green, intricately carved, and next to it were more like it, only in different figures. She glanced about wonderingly.

Then she started. She had caught sight of a strange face, a grotesque at the corner of the ceiling. She stared up at it. It seemed to wink and grimace back at her. She looked at the other corners. Each corner had a grotesque in it, each more hideous than the last. She supposed it must be some fashion of the times, but how odd, she thought, in the midst of all this beauty.

She walked over to the mantel, and examined with pleasure the carvings on the dark wood, the art objects on the marble mantel. When a voice came from behind her, she started.

"Does the room please you, little cousin?" It was Vincent, and she turned to greet him shyly, her cheeks blooming with color.

He was looking grave and stern, but as she looked up at his great height timidly, his face relaxed and he smiled at her.

"Oh, everything is so beautiful, my lord," she said shyly. He tapped her cheek sharply with his finger.

"What is my name?" he asked, sternly.

"V-Vincent," she stammered.

"Yes. Now come to luncheon. If you are a very good girl, I shall show you about the castle and grounds this afternoon. There is a little fantasy on the grounds which may please you. It was made for a small fairy-girl, and you are one such."

This roused her curiosity, and he must have sensed it, because he gave her a teasing look. At luncheon, he entertained her with lively stories about his mother's people. The Caudills, her side of the family, had been active in the wars since the castle had been built, some five hundred years ago, he said. Kings had visited, pirates had raided on the coast, smugglers still operated nearby. He

16

told her there was a view up on a hill near the castle from where she could see the ocean.

"Oh, I should like that enormously!" she said eagerly, sitting up straight. "I have missed the sea—I mean—I thought I should miss it! But if I might see it occasionally—"

"Of course you may! We are but five miles from the sea. Did you think you would see only moors hereabouts? No, the land curves and the sea comes in a distance. You traveled north to me, cousin, but the sea traveled up with you." And he gave her a curious look. "You are like some sea nymph," he mused, gazing at her. "Only—such innocence, and purity—with no sophistication—what do you know of life, I wonder?"

She did not know how to answer him, and gazed at him perplexed. He diverted her by offering her some light white wine chosen especially for her, and she tried it. It was delicate and light, yet it still made her head spin a bit. She was not used to wine, she told him.

"I can see that. It does not displease me. Now, this afternoon, I think we shall walk first about the grounds. Later, I shall show you about the castle, but it is a weary long walk! There are four wings jutting out from the main halls."

"Perhaps I could explore it alone, if I may," she suggested. "I would not take up your time, my l-l— I mean, V-Vi-Vincent."

He shot her a fiery look, then grinned, with a little demon of mischief in his glance. "You will learn to say it without stammering," he told her, with mock gravity. "Practice it a dozen times a day, I advise you!"

After luncheon, Vincent sent for a cloak for her. When Rosa brought the cloak, it was not her shabby grey one. It was a grand one of blue velvet, yet cut just to her size. Adrienne fingered it curiously, then looked at her cousin questioningly. He nodded.

"Yes, it belonged to my mother. She was of your size," he said. He measured himself against her casually. "Just as high as my heart," he said. "You are a tiny thing."

"But I am strong," she assured him earnestly. "I told you I could work hard. And I can, my—my l-l—*Vincent!*"

He caught her small hand and swung it boyishly. "Very well, come along and work, my strong one. You shall walk and learn and study all the afternoon!"

But she thought he was teasing her. For what he did was to take her for a long pleasant walk about the grounds surrounding the grim high towers and turrets of Castle Caudill. The lawns stretched green down to an immense lake. There were black swans on the lake, the first black ones she had ever seen, and she exclaimed in pleasure over them.

Near the lake, he showed her the "fantasy." It was a small house, almost like a doll house. It had but one room, and that so beautifully furnished that she was awed. Silk drapes hung from ceiling to floor. All was ruby red and gold.

"Do you like it?" he asked. "Then it is yours. You shall come here and play whenever you like!"

"But I am not a child," she answered his teasing words. "Indeed, I am quite grown-up!"

"Are you indeed?" he asked, softly. She looked at him to see if he were teasing, and met a fiery look from his flashing green eyes. She felt suddenly warm, uncomfortable, strange, and oddly stifled in the hothouse atmosphere of the room.

They returned to the castle, and he showed her some of the lovely rooms. But she was weary, and he took her back to one of the living rooms for tea, and talked to her in a casual pleasant tone which made her quite forget her strangeness.

During the next few days, she seemed to have no duties at all, but was free to wander about the castle and grounds. Vincent rode out almost daily, seeing to the tenants, he told her when she timidly asked. There were more than five hundred of them, farmers, herdsmen, even some fishermen. He told her about the town nearby, but warned her not to ride there alone.

"For the folks there are rough, and tempers uncertain now. I will tell you about that later," he said, and frowned. "You will be safer to stay close about the castle and grounds, though I shall not confine you, cousin! You are free to explore where you will."

She had been curious about one matter, and asked Rosa. There was no chapel in the castle. Rosa frowned, and finally said, "Oh, miss, don't ask *him* about that. His father grew quite angry with some of the priests, and forbade any chapel services. And truly the priest in town—we don't like him at all! If you must have services, perhaps my lord will take you into a city one day, but don't ask *him* about that now, while he is troubled about matters!"

Adrienne said nothing to Vincent about it. She felt it was little enough to repay his great kindness and generosity toward her. She continued to explore the great castle, and found suites of rooms, great halls and banquet rooms, ballrooms untouched and dusty, paintings hung and tarnished, one wing after another of neglected rooms and furnishings. Only the main hall and the wing where she had her rooms were kept in good order.

One morning she started toward the basement and cellars in her explorations. She had discovered a winding stone staircase which seemed to lead to the wine cellars. And Vincent had said she might explore where she wished.

She turned and twisted with the narrowing stairs, and finally came out in a cool dark cellar, where to her delight and satisfaction she found kegs and bottles of many wines and brandies. Beyond it was another large stone room, and another.

She wondered what might be there, and lifted her skirts to keep them from the dusty floors. But—she leaned down and examined the floors curiously. They were not dusty. They were quite swept clean. And then she heard chanting.

She gasped. It sounded like church services! Could it be? Could Vincent or the servants be having a church in the cellars? Perhaps some of the servants missed their chapel, and had services down here when the master was out.

In growing excitement, she followed the sound, from one room to the next, until abruptly she came out to the door of a huge chapel. She saw the stained glass windows, the sun slanting through them, the huge altar, and people standing about. She thought she recognized the butler, the housekeeper, a maid or two, and others.

Why, why had they not told her? She would have enjoyed participating in the service. Impulsively she started forward, and then the figure at the altar turned and faced to the left.

She put her hand over her mouth to halt the scream which wanted to tear through her throat. The figure was all in black velvet, from head to foot. What she had thought was the robe of a priest was a velvet cloak, and a hood. Over the face was a mask, through which gleamed slits of flashing eyes. He was looking toward a girl, motioning her forward. She hesitated, the white hand made an imperious gesture.

The girl was dressed in a red muslin dress. As she came near the "priest" he reached out his hand, and caught hold of the neck of her dress. As Adrienne gasped, he ripped it from neck to waist, then off her, so that her nude white body was exposed to all their gaze. Adrienne pressed her hand more tightly over her mouth.

The "priest" bent forward, picked up the girl easily, and laid her on the black marble altar. He stretched her out, passing his hands over and over her body, from her feet to her neck, and down over her again. The others stretched forward to see the happenings. He was saying something in a muttering voice. The people swayed as though in a trance. Their bodies twitched.

On the floor, Adrienne noticed now, were painted round circles, symbols of strange design, in gold and red and black. The priest stepped back, motioned to someone. A woman brought a golden vessel like a communion cup. He took it, raised it to his lips, drank. Then he went to the girl on the altar, raised her head, put the cup to her lips. She drank, deeply, drained the cup.

The she lay back. He passed his hands over her body, again, again, and she began to cry out in a strange voice. He took a knife, and before Adrienne's dazed eyes he cut the area over her throat. Blood spurted! He dipped his fingers in the blood, rubbed them on her breasts, on her thighs.

It was too much for Adrienne. Terrified as she was, she found her strength, and fled! She picked up her skirts, and ran back through the huge cellars, to the winding stairs, and up them, running, running, until she gained the sanctuary of her room. She dashed inside, and shut the door. She leaned against the door, panting, haunted, terrified, her breath coming in great gulps from her open mouth.

"Oh—what—what—shall I—do?" she muttered. She pressed her small hand to her heaving breasts. "Oh—what—was he doing—murder—was it murder?"

Something terrible had been happening there. Something about ritual and magic and drugs and a naked girl—and she was terrified. What was it? Then the words came—a black mass! A black mass! A Satanic ritual!

Devil worshipers! She had heard about them from

some fishermen, describing some weird things they had seen in the South Seas on far trips on whaling vessels. Natives, chanting over the nude ripe bodies of young girls, strange ceremonies which made her father furious when he learned she had listened to the stories.

Black mass. Devils and deamons, and Satan being invoked—

Where could she go? To whom could she turn?

The priest—in town. The one they did not like! She thought of it, and clung to the thought.

She would go to the priest, and beg his help. All this beauty and luxury was a trap, she thought, in terror. All the silks and satins and flowers and jewels, all the art objects and paintings—and in the cellars a black mass! With blood spurting!

She shuddered. With an effort she pushed herself away from the door, and went to get the thick blue velvet cloak. She wished she had her own shabby grey one, it would be a comfort to her now, but Vincent had ordered all her old shabby clothes taken away.

Vincent! Did he know about this? Did he let them do this?

She could not answer the question. She closed her mind to it. She swung the blue cloak about her, and crept down the stairs again. Servants saw her, gazed, smiled, and let her go on. The butler opened the great front door for her.

"It's a lovely day," she said, casually.

"Yes, indeed, miss, not a bit of rain in sight," he said.

She walked slowly down the wide stairs, then down to the curving driveway, out to the grounds. She knew in which direction was the town, a footman had pointed it out to her one day. She set out, though it was a distance.

She walked rapidly, fear driving her. In a couple hours, she reached the town. She had thought she might have to ask direction, but when she arrived, she found the huge church easily. Beside it was the parish house, and she knew she would find a priest there.

She went to the door, knocked, and was admitted. In a few minutes, a black-frocked figure came into the room.

The man came smiling toward her, and she felt almost faint with her relief. "I am Father James Francis, my dear. I understand you are Miss Adrienne Caudill, from the castle."

21

His warm hand closed about her small cold hand, and she felt a curious strength in it. She looked up, into his eyes, and thought involuntarily how black they were.

"Oh, yes, Father. I am Miss Caudill. I have come—I have come to tell you—something terrible is happening—" She paused, choking over the words.

A flame seemed to leap into his eyes. "Something terrible?" he asked alertly. "What is it, my dear?" His black eyes were glittering.

She was puzzled, weary, distraught. There was something wrong here. She had thought to come to a man of God, a being wise and strong. She looked at him in his black frock, the turned white collar, with his large white hands, and tried again to speak. "It is—something I saw—something—"

She hesitated again, then burst into tears. she was so upset, so overwrought by what she had seen. He helped her to sit down in a plump velvet chair. It felt like one of the luxurious chairs at the castle, not the plain wooden one like that in the home of the priest she had known in her own village.

"There, there, child. I'll get you a glass of wine, and you shall be able to tell me everything." There was a strange ring of excitement in his tone. He hurried from the room.

Adrienne drew the blue velvet cloak closer about her, shuddering. Something was wrong—some thing—her intuition was affecting her deeply, warning her. She glanced up as a movement caught her eye. A small maid in a long grey dress and a mob cap sidled into the room. Her wide eyes caught Adrienne's attention.

"No, no, don't drink nothing from him," said the girl in a rapid whisper. "Don't drink nothing, dearie! Listen to me—he's in league with a witch! There's a woman who furnishes him drinks, and there's women who does his will when the drink is in them!" She nodded, winked, grinned foolishly.

Adrienne started up with a cry. She felt haunted, driven. Before she could stop herself, she brushed past the maid, and out into the hall, and down the stairs into the fresh outdoors.

She ran out into the narrow streets like a woman possessed. People paused to glance and stare at the small blonde girl in the rich blue velvet cloak, stare and nod wisely at her, because she had come from the priest's house.

She felt their curiosity, and shrank from it. Was there no sanctuary? She paused briefly at the church door, heard chanting. It reminded her vividly of that horrible scene in the cellars, and she turned away shuddering violently.

Was there no place to go? No, no place at all. Not in the village, not in the castle.

Like a wild thing, she raced down the street. Her blonde hair came down from its demure coils, and hung down over the blue cloak. She raced past the apothecary's and the baker's, past the small school where children droned on monotonously, past some curious women with their market baskets. Past donkeys and horses hitched to rails. Past the markets, and past a small inn, and past the edge of town. She was on the way back to the castle before she realized it.

She halted, and looked about in bewilderment. No, she could not return to the castle. She could not think, she was in a daze, cold, in the October chill. Where could she go? Perhaps she could go to the sea! She thought of the sea, her friendly sea, with its moods and colors and lights and haunting sounds. It was in that direction, she felt sure, and she started across the moors.

Soon she was lost. Each hillock looked like every other one. She had lost sight of the town, as dusk came on. And with the dusk, the air darkened and the rains came. Her velvet cloak was soon soaked through.

She trudged on, her head bent. Surely she would soon smell the sea, she thought doggedly.

She could not go back. That was all she knew. She must run, and run. But she was—so—tired—

She would just pause and rest in some shelter for a little time. But there was no shelter. Just another hillock, another bush, another clump of fuzz.

Finally she sank down wearily on the ground, the wet ground, and put her head down on her arms. She would rest—for one—moment—just a—small—moment—then she would—go on—toward the—beautiful peaceful gentle—sea—toward the sea—

CHAPTER 3

"Adrienne! Adrienne!" The voice was low, commanding, deep, near.

The girl wakened from her stupor, stirred on the hard ground, and drew her wet cloak about her with a deep weary shudder. The voice—it had seemed so close! She gazed about her into the darkness, but saw no one.

"Adrienne! Adrienne! Answer me!"

"I am—here—" she muttered. She felt ill, feverish, dazed. She spoke into the darkness, and in the darkness came the answer.

"Speak again, Adrienne! Speak again, I command you!"

"Here—here—I am here," she said, weakly. She sank down again on the ground. She wanted to sleep, to sleep, and not to waken. The horrors she had seen and experienced pressed too close. Life was not welcome.

"Adrienne!" the voice commanded. "This is Vincent. Speak to me, Adrienne!"

"Yes—yes, Vincent—yes, Vince—Vincent—Vincent—"

She pillowed her head on her arm, and tried to doze off. If she slept deeply enough, she might not waken again on this earth. She would waken in heaven, with her dearest mother and her beloved father, and nothing would trouble her ever again—

The voice bothered her again. It was angry, furious, like that cursing voice she had heard at the inn. "Damn it, Adrienne, don't go to sleep. Answer me!"

"Yes, Vincent—yes—Vincent—"

The voice kept bothering her, calling her, wakening her. She mumbled, had to answer it. Then she heard the hard stamp of a horse nearby. The voice commanded it to halt. Someone came to her.

"Adrienne!" He was bending over her, he scooped her up in his hard arms. He was enraged, his face glowering in the darkness. His eyes seemed to shoot fiery sparks, burning her. "How dared you run off from me!" He

24

bent his head, pressed his lips to her cheek. The touch burned her cheek. She turned her face, whimpering in fright.

She felt a strange mixture of feelings as he carried her back to the waiting black stallion. She felt delivered into evil, held tightly in his angry arms, the prey caught and held in hard hands. Yet she felt safe, warmed, rescued, all at once. She was bewildered, and too weary to sort out her feelings.

He managed to get into the saddle, still holding her, and settled her into his arms. He lifted his own thick warm cloak about her, sheltering her from the rain and chill. He was still muttering curses. "Damn it to hell—this black night and rain—what possessed you, Adrienne? Why did you run off from me?"

He was furiously angry with her, she felt it in the tightness of his grip, the coldness of his tone, the heat of his lips as he touched her cheek.

"I was—so frightened," she muttered. "So—frightened—"

"Frightened?" he asked sharply. "Why? What did you see? What happened?"

"I saw—saw a black mass—down in the cellars—oh, Vincent, a girl was murdered—I saw her—on a black altar—the priest was not a priest—oh, I am so—frightened," and she began to shudder again, and to weep, in little whimpering sobs.

He gathered her up against him, against the heat of his strong body, and soothed her. "Little angel, little one, don't cry, we will soon be home. You are feverish. Come, don't cry, don't weep, my little angel, hush, hush—"

He was gentle with her, abruptly, as though reining in his own fury to soothe her. The horse started at the touch of his heel and the command of his voice, and Vincent rode like the devil with her. The wind seemed to whistle about them, but she lay in a daze in his arms, little heeding anything about her.

At the steps to the castle, he slid down, still holding her, and let the groom take the horse. He carried her up the long stairs, up and up, and it reminded her of that first night she had come, only this was different.

Now she was not going into a strange castle, her future home. She had the haunted feeling she was being carried back into imprisonment, into a horrible future, into strangeness and terror such as she had never known.

25

And she could not even struggle. She was caught tight in a strange trap, held tightly by the man she liked, yet feared.

Did Vincent know about the black masses in the cellar, did he condone it, did he let them do it? Did he know about the murders? The throat slashing of a tender young girl?

Did he know? Did he—sometimes—attend? Was he one of them?

She was shuddering violently by the time they reached the great stone hall, where iron and black weapons hung on the walls, reminders of the grim past of five hundred years of wars and fighting. The red banners hung like flames on the grey stone. To her fevered imagination the stone torches flickered like the bonfires of the devil.

Mrs. Griffith came to meet them, her face anxious. "Oh, you have the poor little dear! Where was she, the love?"

"On the moors," said Vincent curtly. Adrienne glanced up at his dark face, at his flashing green eyes. "She was lost on the moors."

Mrs. Griffith helped Vincent remove Adrienne's soaked blue velvet cloak. "Upstairs with her," said Vincent. "Hot soaking bath, and into bed. Hot tea and rum."

"Oh, yes, my lord," said Mrs. Griffith. She trotted after them as Vincent swung Adrienne up again into his arms and fairly ran with her up the winding stairs. He carried her along the hallway, scowling ahead of them, to her rooms.

In her rooms, he carried her right into her bathroom. She thought he even might stay and undress her! She would faint with shame if he did so, she thought, in anguish. But Rosa was soon there, and Vincent left her to the two women.

They stripped off her wet clothes, and popped her into a steaming hot bath. By this time she was hot and moaning and raving about black masses, and devils, and a girl murdered, and Rosa and Mrs. Griffith were shaking their heads over her.

"Fevered," muttered Mrs. Griffith. "She is in for some sickness, I'll warrant!"

"Poor little dear," said Rosa, compassionately. She was scrubbed and scoured and warmed, and rinsed, then lifted out bodily, and dried, then put into a warm woolen gown.

26

They fairly carried her into bed, and tucked the covers about her warmly.

She settled down into the covers to sleep, but kept muttering and moaning. She did not want to sleep, she fought it. In her dreams, she might see again the horrors she had just experienced.

The women whispered. Presently Vincent came, holding a tall silver cup. He bent over her. "Adrienne, you must drink this, it will help you sleep."

She looked up at him, her blue eyes fever-bright and vacant. She just saw his dark scowling face, the flashing green eyes, the jut of his aggressive black pointed beard, the darkness of his black hair. "No, no, no, I don't want to sleep," she whispered. "I am frightened, I am frightened."

He bent, and put his long arm about her thin shoulders, and lifted her from the pillows. "Drink, child," he said, and his voice was more gentle. "Tomorrow I will scold you for running off like that. Tonight, I will be nice to you, only you must do as I command you!"

She sighed deeply, too weak to fight his will. She opened her mouth obediently. He put the cup to her lips. She swallowed, and half choked over the hot mixture of tea and something that smelled strange. "Drink again," he said, forcefully, and put the cup to her.

She had to drink the whole cup to the bottom. By this time her head was whirling and odd, the pictures in her mind blurring and fading. She leaned back against his solid arm, her eyes closing without her willing them to. She was so hot, so ill, so mixed-up. Vincent's large warm hand stroked gently over her wet blonde hair, and he brushed it back from her forehead with a soothing gesture.

"There, there, little one, now you will sleep," he murmured, his tone soothing her. It was monotonous, yet resonant and deep. "You will sleep, and rest, and tomorrow you will be better. You will sleep, close your eyes and sleep, sleep, sleep. You will have dreams—of the blue sea you love, and blue flowers the color of your eyes, you will dream of roses and their fragrant perfume. You will think of islands with palm trees waving in the wind—the scent of flowers—all things lovely—scents like incense and perfume—sleep, Adrienne, sleep, and dream of beauty and gentle things—kittens curled in their basket —softness like velvet—sleep, Adrienne. Dream of roses,

27

and perfume, and the blue sea, and the salt wind in your face, then a fresh breeze off the coast—"

She sighed, and turned her face against him, and finally slept. She could still feel his hand stroking her hair when she drifted off into the perfumed dreams he had commanded her to know.

The next few days she was so ill and feverish she knew very little. She was only vaguely aware of the maid Rosa lifting her, sponging her body, putting fresh night garments on her. She knew the voice several times of Mrs. Griffith, saying, "Poor little dear one, poor little one—"

She was more aware when Vincent came, and lifted a cup to her lips, and commanded her forcefully to drink. She tried to turn her face from the cup, he held her chin, and swore at her, and told her to drink or he would beat her!

"Now, sir," said Mrs. Griffith, gently. "The little dear is ill—"

"Not too ill to disobey me!" he said, with grim anger.

Adrienne caught his slim powerful wrist in her hot fingers, and looked up at him imploringly. "Oh, my lord, do not make me drink—that stuff," she whispered. "I am frightened, I am frightened—"

His face came down close to hers, his eyes gleamed with anger. "Frightened—of me?"

"Yes—sir—yes—" she whispered, and closed her eyes against his anger. He lifted her in his arm from the pillow and set the cup commandingly to her lips.

"But drink anyway," he said, his tone very hard. And she drank. She slept, and dreamed again. Sometimes the dreams were pleasant, of palms, and roses and fragrance. But sometimes she saw again the black altar, the nude body of the writhing girl, the lifted dagger, the red blood spurting, and she would cry out.

Finally one morning, she woke to the sunshine streaming in her windows, turning to molten gold across the cream satin spread. She moved her hands on the bedspread, and lifted them, and marveled at their thinness. She could see the blue veins clearly, and the redness and roughness were gone. Her white hands were as frail as she had ever seen them.

But the fever and heat were gone. She felt alert and alive once more. The dreams were gone, vanished. She sat up slowly, and felt much more herself.

28

"Rosa?" she called out tentatively. Many times she had called in fright, and Rosa had come.

The middle-aged woman appeared at once. She beamed down at the small girl in the middle of the huge bed. "There, now, dear, you look more the thing!" she said comfortably. "I shall bring you some hot tea, then you shall have a hot bath, and we shall see how we are!"

Adrienne giggled. It struck her funny that Rosa should see how *we* are, when the maid was obviously in the best of health. Rosa laughed with her, pleased that she was laughing, and went for tea.

When Adrienne had had her bath, she was dressed in a lovely set of silk underclothes, and a long blue negligee of frills and lace and settled on her small cream velvet sofa. It just fit her, with cushions at her back and at her side. Rosa spread a plump satin coverlet over her to keep her warm, and brought her some breakfast, hot tea, hot biscuits, an egg, thick creamy butter and a small pot of jam.

Adrienne ate with pleasure. She was so hungry. As she was finishing a hot biscuit, Vincent strode in. He was tall, looming in the room, his black hair and black jutting beard and black morning clothes making him look very formidable. She stared up at him, her heart beginning to beat uncomfortably.

He came over, to loom over her. "So, little cousin, you are feeling better this morning."

"Yes, much better, thank you, my l-l-l—" She had to hesitate, gulp at the scowl on his face. "Thank you, Vincent," she finished meekly.

"And your nightmares are over?" he asked, his scowl gradually fading, though his green eyes flashed as before. He sat down on the small plump chair at her side, and put his fingers on her wrist. "Yes, your hand is cool this morning. Good."

She moved her small hand in his hold, wriggled it until she could timidly grasp his fingers. "I wish to th-thank you, my—Vincent—because you have been so—good to me. I don't know what I said—in my nightmares—" She hesitated. She had a vague recollection of screaming out at him that he was a demon and she was afraid of him. She flushed, looked up at him appealingly.

"You were ill, very ill," he said, finally. He was still angry, she thought, but his tone was quieter. He clasped her fingers strongly, held them as though he would not

29

let them go. She let them lie passively in his, she could not fight him, he was much too strong. "Now, tell me, why did you go out on the moors? Why did you run away?"

Her lashes drooped, uneasily, she turned her face from his. He insisted, and in a low tone, she finally told him what she had witnessed. He was silent when she had finished. Rosa was working quietly at the other end of the bedroom.

She finally asked, "What was it—Vincent? What did I see?" She looked up at him, her wide eyes troubled. "What was in the cellars?"

"You were ill," he said, quietly. The blaze in his eyes had died down. "You were already feverish. You saw nothing, I believe. Nothing at all. It was your imagination."

She stared at him, unbelieving. He looked right back at her, so positive, so sure, that her own thoughts began to waver. Could it be true? Had she been ill, so feverish that she had imagined everything? She frowned, puzzled. He reached out, and smoothed the delicate line of her eyebrows with a teasing finger.

"You will believe it soon, little cousin," he said, with the old tormenting tone. "There is much fever in the air, and you have caught something. Why, you were very ill for more than a week!"

She was troubled, but he remained and talked to her of other matters. He told her if she was a good girl, he would take her down to the fantasy in the garden the next day, and let her play there. She protested spiritedly, that she was not a child, and he only laughed at her.

"Why, if I offered to tell you a fairy story, you would accept at once!" he teased her, his eyes watching her face.

Her eyes widened. "Oh—do you know a fairy story?" she asked, eagerly.

He put his hand on the back of her neck, affectionately, and shook her a little. "Of course, I do. Now, listen. Once, there was a green mermaid. She was green from the tips of her little toes, to the long green hair which she spread on the rocks at the edge of the sea. One day—" And he began the story, and in spite of the teasing mocking light in his eyes, she could not restrain her eagerness and delight in his story. It was woven with great skill, told easily, with magic in his tone and the words.

After that, he told her other stories, and entertained her with his adventures abroad, and tales of his mother's family. He stayed with her the entire day, having luncheon with her in her room, until he finally told her with great determination that now she would lie down and rest until evening. She protested.

"Yes, you shall," he said. "For if you are very good, I shall let you come down to dinner with me this evening. So, into bed you go," and he picked her up from the sofa, and laid her down in the middle of her great bed. He pressed a careless kiss on her cheek, a cool caress, like one would give a child, she thought, and he left her.

To her surprise, she did sleep, wakening at dusk, to be dressed in a rose-colored muslin gown. Rosa put a great creamy cashmere shawl about her shoulders before she would take her down to the dining room.

At dinner, Vincent greeted her with mock ceremony, seated her at his side, and proceeded to entertain her again with more stories. "For you are a child, after all, and I must fill your lively head with better stories than those of witches and demons that you insist on thinking up!"

"But I did see—and hear—" she began indignantly.

He leaned over, and deliberately took her small chin in his hands and put his warm lips on her soft untutored lips. He pressed them firmly. Then he lifted his head and laughed down at her.

"If you say such things again, I shall silence you—like that," he threatened, his eyes flashing and mocking. She gazed up at him dumbly. Her heart was beating very fast. She did not know if she was frightened—or very excited.

Later he spoke of his mother. She dared to ask, "Vincent, where is your mother buried? Is there a cemetery on the grounds?"

A shadow passed over his dark face, hardening it. "No, she lies in the crypt in the cellars. Sometime, when you are quite over your fevers and imagination, I shall take you down there. Would you like to place flowers on her crypt, little one?"

"Yes, please, I should like that," she said, simply. "It will be like—placing flowers on the grave of my own dear mother. And your father, Vincent, is he—there—also?"

"You will see his crypt beside hers," he answered. And then he reached out and pressed her hand gently where it lay on the table. "Why such dark thoughts, little one? Aren't you happy with me?"

"Oh, yes, yes, I am," she said, hurriedly. "I never thought—to have such care—such comfort. I do appreciate it, cousin!"

"Good. Then you may thank me by having no more terrible thoughts! I want you to be happy always with me."

She bent her head over the beautiful cut glass cup of chocolate custard which he had ordered for her dessert. She spooned the delicate whipped cream thoughtfully to her mouth, licked the little silver spoon thoughtlessly, then glanced up to see his eyes laughing at her childishness. She blushed.

After dinner, he took her to the living room which she had told him was her favorite. The blue and gold of the room soothed and pleased her. He had her to sit with her feet up on a blue sofa, and he set a small table at her side. Then he brought several objects over to her.

"I shall tell you stories about each one of them," he said, and placed a round carved ivory ball in her hand to begin. On the table he had set a jade figurine, of a lady in a strange style of dress, a Japanese lady, he told her. Beside the lady was a round porcelain egg, very gilded and elaborate; when opened it revealed a golden coach, from Russia, he said. The largest object was a carved wooden box, and when he opened it a tune came stealing out into the room, a small tinkling pretty melody.

She was enchanted with the objects, and his stories of them. But all the time she was thinking about his words, "I want you to be happy always with me." What did he mean? Did he not mean to help her obtain a governess post somewhere? What work could she do in his huge castle, crowded with hundreds of servants, or on his estate, with his five hundred tenants? She puzzled and puzzled about it, and could not decide what work she could do to help him. Surely he did not mean for her to live here always. He was just being kind because she was ill.

After he had talked to her for a time, he told her she was weary, and must go to bed early. "Then tomorrow, I might allow you to venture outdoors, only it must

32

be a warm day, and you may go out only with me, my little stubborn one!"

He took her up to her room, saw her inside her door, then pressed the little porcelain egg into her hand. "This is for you to keep, little angel. A toy to play with, my child!" And he laughed at her protesting face, and kissed her cheek warmly. He left her, and closed the door.

When he had left, and she had pressed the little gold object in her hands for a moment, she suddenly realized she had not thanked him for the gift. "Oh, how thoughtless," she whispered.

She opened the door. She could hear Rosa stirring in her bedroom, laying out the night garments. She said, quietly, "Vincent?" He was just going down the hall, she could see his back—only, she frowned—he was wearing a black velvet cloak!

Had Vincent gone to his room, put on a cloak, and returned?

She called to him, stepping out into the hall, walking after him down the long corridor. "Vincent! Oh, Vincent, I did not thank you for the darling porcelain egg—Vincent?"

The neat black head turned. She saw the jutting beard, the arrogant pose. The black velvet cloak swung as the man turned about. She found herself staring into black flashing eyes, a coldly arrogant face. Vincent—but not Vincent!

She stared, then her hand went to her lips. No, it was not Vincent! The man stared down at her, from a distance of some ten feet, he looked at her from her head to her toes, and back up again. He was frowning, his head erect, his black eyes sparkling with some strange light. He was a little older than Vincent, she thought.

But who could he be? For an instant, she thought he might be Vincent's father. But Vincent's father, the late Lord of Castle Caudill, lay buried in the crypt beside his wife!

The man stared at her, a long arrogant stare. Then he waved a white hand impatiently. He walked toward the side of the hall, then before her staring eyes—he walked—through—the wall—and was gone!

"Oh—no—no—" she whispered, her hand pressing tightly to her lips. The porcelain ball in her small hand felt suddenly heavy. She ran to her room, shut the door, and leaned, panting and panicky, against the heavy carved wood.

She had seen—something—something not of this world. And she was frightened—cold and frightened.

CHAPTER 4

Adrienne thought she would not sleep that night, but she did somehow. Her dreams were filled with Vincent, in a black velvet cloak, only his eyes were green and gentle, and he laughed as he told her stories. Comforted, she pressed her cheek to the little porcelain egg she had taken to bed with her, and when she wakened, she was able to sleep again.

Rosa pronounced her much better the next morning. She was bathed and dressed in a new dress. "Oh, where did this come from, Rosa?" Adrienne exclaimed, fondling the soft blue cashmere of the fabric. It was so warm and so soft, as soft as a lamb. "Is this more from the wardrobe of the lady?"

"No, dearie, my lord sent for clothes from London, and they have arrived! He gave me this for you to wear today. And such dresses, of the finest muslins and silks and satins! And the dear pretty cloaks, and bonnets and shawls and little slippers! Oh, wait till you see them, my dear!" And Rosa beamed down at her.

"He—sent to London—for clothes—for me?" Adrienne stared up at her.

"Of course, love. Dozens of clothes. But you are to see them only one at a time, he said, for surprises!" And the maid giggled with pleasure. "Wait till you see your beautiful dress for dinner tonight!"

"But—but Rosa, he should not have—I mean—I shall not be here long. I must obtain a post somewhere—perhaps as a governess," she added wistfully. Her hand smoothed lovingly over the blue cashmere fabric, as Rosa settled her on the cream velvet sofa, and put the satin spread over her lower body.

"Oh, my dear, he will not let you go away," said Rosa, simply, and tucked the spread about her legs warmly. "There, dear, are you quite comfortable?"

"Yes—yes, quite." Adrienne leaned back into the cushions, puzzled and troubled. He would not let her go away? What did Rosa mean? Did he mean to spoil her and treat her as a true close cousin, and keep her here forever? Or was some deeper meaning there?

Vincent arrived with her breakfast. He dropped a kiss carelessly on her blonde curls, arranged to her shoulders, not like her usual neat braids. "There, you look quite yourself today, my dearest! Are you ready to go outdoors for a small time?"

She smiled up at him, glad that he was gay and happy this morning, not dark and scowly with that hard expression on his scarred face. "Oh, I should like that immensely, Vincent. And—and may I thank you for the darling pretty dress? And my lovely porcelain egg? I took it to bed with me last night," she confided childishly.

He laughed aloud, and seated himself on the plump chair near her sofa. "Did you indeed? How lucky was the porcelain egg! Do you like the color of your dress?" he went on swiftly, before she could puzzle out his remark.

She smoothed her hand over the fabric. "Oh, so much. It is as blue as the sea on a calm sunny day. And so soft—like a little lamb."

Rosa set her tea before her, in the delicate blue and white china cup. Vincent, without asking her, added thick cream and spoonsful of sugar to her cup, and set it to her hand. He watched with great satisfaction as she ate an egg and some ham, hot biscuits and honey and butter.

When she had eaten, he said, "Good girl. I shall take you out to the fantasy this morning, and settle you there. You can do with some fresh air, and though it is late October the air is mild today."

He sent Rosa for her cloak. When it came, it was not the blue velvet, but a deeper blue and gold plaid that made her exclaim with delight. He watched her with a smile as it was set about her.

"Yes, I thought that color would match your eyes," he said. "Your eyes are not a pale blue, they are deep and vivid."

"And her pretty hair the color of the gold," said Rosa, touching the long blonde curls fondly.

"Yes, I like that style much better," said Vincent critically, studying it. "I told Rosa to dress it that way, Adrienne. I think it becomes you better than the tight way you did it."

She opened her mouth to protest, found he was looking at her with amusement and some warning in his green eyes. She closed her mouth again. If it pleased him to order her clothes and her hair style, it was probably little enough, for all he was doing for her, she thought.

He took her out to the fantasy, holding her about the waist as though she might fall. They walked slowly along the garden paths. The late October winds had blown many of the leaves from the trees, but today was so warm that the black swans sailed serenely on the blue lake, and only a few white clouds were reflected on their surface. She drew deep happy breaths.

At the fantasy, he opened one of the windows for her, settled her on a red sofa, put a crimson rug over her knees. She cuddled down, and looked up at him questioningly. Would he tell her stories, or amuse her with his jokes, or tease her, or what?

A footman followed them into the fantasy, carrying a small pile of leather-bound books. Vincent motioned for him to set them down on a table beside the sofa.

"I find I must ride out today, little cousin," he said. "You must promise to be a good girl, and stay quiet. I have some books for you to read. I do not want you to take any from my cases, there are some not suitable for you to read! But I shall choose books for you from time to time, and you shall tell me afterwards what you enjoy."

She picked up the first book, and exclaimed. It was a book of poetry by one of her favorite authors. "Oh, I shall enjoy this, Vincent. Do not trouble yourself about me. I can read all day. Thank you!" She sent a glowing happy smile up at his dark face. It lightened a little, and the eyes seemed not so moody and unhappy.

Another footman came in, carrying a huge armful of flowers. Vincent nodded at him, and he began to set the flowers in vases about the room. Adrienne gazed at them with great pleasure. There were huge red roses, small creamy roses, a vivid blue flower she did not know, a strange purple one, a black flower streaked with gold. Vincent took this last one and put it in her hand.

"This is an orchid, my dear. Do you like it?" He was watching her closely. She put it to her nose, sniffed it, wrinkled her nose.

"I do not smell anything, Vincent," she said, puzzled.

"Not all flowers are fragrant," he said, and there seemed to be some hidden significance to his voice. "You will learn to like many beautiful objects you have not known before. For now—" He took the orchid from her, and set it on a nearby table. He studied the flowers the footman had arranged, chose a creamy small rose, and put this in her hand. She sniffed it, was delighted, smiled, and tucked it in the front of her dress.

He left her with a careless admonition not to stir far away. She settled down with the book of poetry, and began to read it with great delight. Every now and then, she glanced up and about the strange exotic red and gold and black room, or out the window toward the blue lake and black swans, thinking about her new life here, puzzling about the many strange things she had seen.

Presently, she was stirred with a desire to write poetry. It always helped to clear her mind, and calm her. She looked about for paper and pen, but none was in the small glorious room. She would go back to the house, to the *castle*, she corrected herself with a little grimace, and obtain paper and pen, and write some lines to comfort herself.

She put on the beautiful new cloak and left the fantasy to walk back to the castle. She walked a new way, and passed by flower beds she had not noticed before. Gardeners were busy, digging up bulbs against the next summer, laying in new ones for spring. They glanced up at her, nodded shyly, ducked their heads down when she spoke to them.

This way led her near the stables. She glanced admiringly at the open doors, at the dozen stalls of handsome horses, greys, blacks, one chestnut brown who tossed his head at her. Then she heard the cursing.

She froze. The voice was Vincent's. The tone was the deadly furious cursing she had heard before. She heard the words, and winced. He was cursing someone in a terrible way.

"Bastard—poaching—damn fool. I warned you! I'll whip the life out of you this time, damn your soul to hell!"

37

She came out of her horrified trance. She picked up her skirts, and without pausing to think, she ran into the stable yard, around past the horses, to where a coach and a carriage were set in the cobblestoned way. A man cringed near Vincent, Vincent had his whip lifted to strike.

She had just time to see the desperate look on the thin haggard face of the middle-aged man, the hard fury of Vincent's face, the rabbits flung on the cobblestones with blood staining their white fur. The servants stood about, mouths agape, unable to move closer to the scene. She saw the head groom scowling.

She ran to Vincent, caught at his arm with her small hands, and gasped, "Oh, no, Vincent, Vincent, do not strike him! He must be very hungry—"

Vincent paused, gazing down at her in absolute incredulity, his green eyes seeming to shoot red fires at her. She knew, with a horror that shook her, that he was furious beyond reasoning. But she braved his look, and gradually his eyes calmed. The hard muscles in his arm relaxed, and he lowered his arm.

"How dare you interfere?" he asked, in a soft deadly tone, glaring down at her.

"I—I had to—he is hungry, Vincent. He would not have—poached—on your—property—he would not have dared—if he were not hungry—and his family—" She gasped out the words, knowing how it was from times in her own village. She had always felt so desperately sorry for the hungry men driven to poaching to feed their families.

Vincent glared at the cringing man, who lifted his head with some show of spirit. "Are you hungry?" asked Vincent, in a cold cutting tone. "What about the cows you had? The chickens? Where are they?"

"The priest cursed them, my lord, and they died," said the man simply. "I told him I could not leave your employ, and he cursed them, and my wife, and my children, and my land. It has not prospered since."

The two men stared at each other, in a long stunned silence.

"The priest—cursed you?" asked Vincent, in a very odd tone.

"Yes, sir. My son—he be a smart one for no schooling—" And there was an odd defensive pride in his tone. "He told the priest he did not believe his teachings, that he was evil for what he done. And the priest, he cursed us all."

"Oh, that was a terrible thing to do!" said Adrienne in a small indignant voice.

Vincent turned and looked down full at her. "He may be lying, my girl," he said, with cruelty. "Would you like to go with me, and catch him in his lying?"

She caught her breath, staring up into his hard face. The scar seemed to glow red on his bronze cheek, against his black hair.

"Yes, I would like—to go—" she said faintly.

He nodded curtly. The head groom gave orders, the carriage was caught up with two black matched horses. The man waited in grim proud silence, his face set. Vincent handed Adrienne into the carriage, got up himself, then hesitated. "You—get on the box with the groom," he said curtly, to his tenant. The man got up. Vincent nodded at one of the men. He tossed the rabbits up to the man, who grabbed them, as though surprised, and clutched the bloody rabbits to his shabby torn coat.

Vincent was silent on the ride. Adrienne dared not speak, the tenant did not turn his head, but sat proudly erect. Adrienne noticed his thinness, his gauntness. He could not be lying.

It was not far to the home of the tenant, a cottage on the edge of the moors. Adrienne noticed that the home was neat, though shabby, the roof was mended with thatch, the chicken runs were neat though empty. Vincent looked about him with a frown, as he handed Adrienne down from the carriage.

A woman came out from the cottage, moving slowly, hesitantly. She stared first at her man, then Vincent, then for a long surprised look at Adrienne.

"But she—my lady—" she began to stammer.

Vincent said curtly, "What do you say?"

The woman gasped, "My lord—I did but think—for a moment—it was the Lady Guinevere returned. But it could not be—she be dead these many years—but she looks so—"

Adrienne smiled at her, suddenly, with a bright glowing look. The woman stared again.

"And her smile—oh, my lord—she is my lady to the life!"

Her husband tried to hush her nervously. Vincent had softened, strangely. He waved his white hand imperiously. "It is all right, I have long noted the resemblance. This is my little cousin, Miss Adrienne Caudill, come to live at the castle. Her mother was second cousin to my mother, Lady Guinevere. The likeness is most amazing, is it not?"

A tall boy came around the edge of the cottage, followed by a younger girl carrying a smaller girl. All were thin, gaunt, their faces aged by hunger. Adrienne was seized with pity, and caught Vincent's arm. "Oh, Vincent," she whispered, into his ear, and he bent his head to her to catch the words. "They are hungry, they are starving! Do but observe their faces and forms! Oh, the poor darlings!!"

He nodded curtly, frowning. He drew her with him, back to the empty chicken runs, out to the pasture where no cows stood. The man was explaining wearily, as though with little hope, how the priest had cursed his stock, and all had sickened and died.

The boy spoke up, spiritedly, "It was not the cursing, father! I have talked to farmers, and others have died. It is something in the grass in our pasture. I tried to tell you this!"

The father shrugged, and turned apologetically to Vincent. "The boy will think and think on these matters, my lord. I do not know. All I know is that they lived for a long time in my care, and now they are dead, and the priest had cursed them."

Vincent bent down, plucked some of the grasses, smelled them. To Adrienne's surprise, he then plucked something else in the grass, looked closely at it, tasted it, spit it out. He frowned.

The boy watched him eagerly, his eyes glowing with interest. Adrienne smiled at him, he hesitated, then returned her smile. Vincent caught their looks, gazed oddly at Adrienne.

"Your boy is right," he finally said, curtly. "The priest has no such powers of darkness. It is the grass which has killed them. This weed is spreading. It must be stopped. Let me see your other pasture. If the weed is not there, you may get cows and put them in it. Then this pasture must be burned, the weed dug up and burned completely. When it is clear, it may be put in grass again, and cows put in it. But first I must be sure the weed is gone."

The tenant seemed to turn to stone. He gazed and gazed at Vincent incredulously. Vincent turned abruptly, as though angry, and took Adrienne's hand, and led her back to the carriage. Adrienne put her other hand urgently on his hand as he would have handed her in. "Vincent—please—there is so much food at the castle. Might not some be sent to them—enough for a few days? Some tea and meat—" She gazed up pleadingly at him.

His face softened. He shook his head, but smiled. "Ah—just like my mother. She would ever try to make me do good," he said oddly. "Very well—this time. It shall be ordered." He turned to the tenant's wife, and said curtly, aloud, "Food shall be sent to you from the castle. Also more chickens for the run. Have your son clear out all trace of the weed first, and burn it down."

The tenant found his voice, "Thank you, thank you, my lord!" He nudged his dumbfounded wife, and she added her thanks. As they began to drive away, the woman called after them.

"And God bless you both, my lord, and miss! God bless you!"

Adrienne smiled back at her, and waved her small hand. Vincent was scowling, and he had seemed to wince at the words. Spoiled naughty man, she thought, tenderly. He hated to be caught doing something good, and she tucked her small hand daringly into his arm.

"Vincent?" she said, and rubbed her cheek against his arm. She felt the tautness of it, and wondered, but was too eager to say what she wished. "That boy—oh, if he could be educated—it would be such a good thing! He is intelligent. If he could read and write, and learn things, what a fine man he will be!"

"Where would a tenant's brat go to school?" said Vincent, in a harsh voice. "And why?"

"Because he is an intelligent boy, and will be a good man," she said quietly, and continued to rub her cheek against his hard arm as the horses trotted along the country lane. "Please—Vincent—you could send him to school!"

"Oh—very well," he said, so roughly and so impatiently, that she could not believe the words for a minute. She stared up at him, and slowly, unwillingly he smiled. "Very well, Adrienne, he shall go to school! And it is all your fault! You make me do good in spite of myself!"

"Oh, the good is in you, Vincent," she said, thankfully. She relaxed in the circle of his arm. "Look how good you have been to me!"

41

"I was but doing what pleased me," he said. He leaned back and looked down at her in a strange way. She kept gazing back at him because she could not look away from the green eyes. "Adrienne—I want you to marry me. Immediately."

She went stiff, her eyes opening in alarm. "What, sir?" she asked, stupidly, after a minute.

"I want you to marry me," he repeated. "You are— the one I want. I knew it the first day. I love you, I adore you. I will make life as easy and beautiful for you as any man on earth can do for the lady he adores. You shall have flowers, and sunshine, and lovely clothes, and jewels, books, ornaments—whatever you ask—except your freedom from me! You shall be mine, absolutely, and do whatever I wish!"

For some reason, she felt a thrill, then a weird fright. He phrased it so oddly, she thought. Do whatever he wished! What did he wish of her? She was so puzzled that she was silent, and he tipped her face back with his finger on her chin. His brilliant green eyes studied her face, and the mixture of emotions on it.

"Well? Well?" he asked impatiently, his face hardening, the scar glowing red. "Will you marry me soon, then, little one? Are you woman enough to marry me? Or are you still a child?" And his mouth came down on hers.

The kiss was hard, demanding, possessive, hot. Her lips felt stilled and soft under his hard strength. She could not move, she was stifled and scared. When he finally raised his head, she drew in her breath, and it was like a sob.

"Will you marry me, then, Adrienne?"

"Oh—sir—I cannot—oh, sir—"

"Yes, you shall," he said, more quietly. "You will think about it a little time, then you shall," and his arm closed about her more tightly.

They reached home, and he led her back to the castle's drawing room. It was past time for luncheon. His mood seemed to have changed abruptly. He was wildly gay and funny, and he made her laugh with his stories all during luncheon. He teased her, tapped her cheek, called her child, but all the time his green eyes studied her, and they were fever-bright.

In the afternoon, she retreated to the fantasy, where she tried to read, and to write poetry for a time. But at

42

tea-time, he invaded her retreat, had tea brought to them both, and in the soft intimate atmosphere of the red and gold and black room, he kissed her face and pressed her to him, his arm tight about her. She was afraid, and struggled to get free of him.

He was so moody, so changeable. When he was gentle and teased her, she liked him. But when he cursed, and his wild passions rose, he frightened her badly.

He sat with her in the circle of his arm, after they had finished tea, and kept pressing kisses on her cheeks. "You are so delicious, so young and naive. I shall teach you many things, my little one, and you shall learn to enjoy them." He turned her face to his, deliberately, and bent to her mouth.

His lips were burning hot and possessive on hers. She felt strangely when his hands roamed over her soft body, and press. on her rounded little breasts, and moved down to her thighs. She felt uneasy, troubled, excited, yet instinct warned her of danger.

"Oh—sir—let us go back to the drawing room—and you shall—tell me—stories—about some of the little—treasures—" she managed to say between his kisses.

He drew back, and laughed harshly. "You like my fantasies, little one? Not reality? Well, you shall learn differently. When we are married, you will learn not to draw back from me, but to press close, and lean your little body to mine—" and he pulled her suddenly, roughly close, so that his hot body seemed to burn all down hers. She moaned, and when he let her go, she put her face in her hands. She felt tears in her eyes.

Presently they returned to the castle, and he let her go to her room. Rosa brought a new beautiful gown proudly for her to wear that evening. It was of a sheer lace and muslin, the bodice low and daring, showing Adrienne's white skin, cut much deeper than any dress she had ever worn. In distress she gazed at herself in the mirror, as Rosa finished doing her hair.

"It is—so low, Rosa. Are you sure this is the fashion?" She studied the white dress, the white breasts half-revealed so daringly, the little white roses bordering the bodice.

"Oh, yes, my lady, the very latest fashion." Rosa deftly turned another curl so it hung to Adrienne's white bare shoulder. She brought a strand of pearls, and set them about Adrienne's creamy throat. The pearls were a faint pink cast, dainty and small. Adrienne touched them uneasily. She had never had any jewelry to wear, and she had a feeling these were most expensive. More pearls were brought for her small ears, and hung almost to her throat. And another pearl was brought, a ring for her finger, and Rosa set it on her right hand. Bracelets were added, until Adrienne felt quite overwhelmed.

Rosa brought the creamy cashmere shawl and set it about her. "Oh, my lady, when London sees you it will be all agog," she said proudly.

"London?" asked Adrienne incredulously.

"Oh, yes, my lady, for surely my lord will take you to London soon after you marry!"

"M-m-marry?" Adrienne gasped, her blue eyes huge.

"Yes, my lady. My lord says he intends to marry you quite soon. May I wish you every happiness, my lady?"

When Adrienne descended the wide staircase, she had a feeling she was going down, down, down into a silk and velvet trap. Vincent was waiting for her at the foot of the stairs, his black evening garb relieved only by the glowing red rubies at his chest, and the huge red ruby ring on his right hand. He lifted that hand to her imperiously, and she had to take it as she descended the last steps. He looked down at her frowningly, critically, then lifted off the cashmere shawl, and tossed it to a nearby footman.

"You shall have wine tonight," he said. "That will warm you. The shawl covers the dress too much." His eyes were on her white throat, the white breasts daringly revealed by the low bodice. She knew she was crimson with embarrassment at his look.

Silently she put her hand on his arm and he led her in to dinner. He was as good as his word, and red wine was set at her place. She sipped at it timidly, found it very strong, but the warmth did tingle in her veins in a few minutes. She was able to relax and talk, and laugh a little at his stories. And always the jade eyes, hard and possessive, were watching her.

The next day, he proposed to her again. When she refused, he became furious, cursed, and walked away from her, leaving her for the morning. When he returned at noon, he was so hard and glowering it frightened her. "If you do not learn to obey me, I shall have to beat you," he said once.

She did not know if he meant it or not.

The next day, a tenant came to see her. The butler came to her in the morning room where she sat trying to write a poem, and begged pardon for disturbing her.

"It is a young person, a female," he said. "And she will speak to you. She will not go away, miss!"

Puzzled, Adrienne asked that the woman be sent in. She sat up straight, and waited. A woman a little older than she walked in hesitantly, stared at her, then dared to smile timidly.

Adrienne smiled back, frankly. She was ordinarily a friendly person. "Who are you? And why do you want to see me?" she asked, curiously.

The girl bobbed a curtsey to her, gracefully. "Oh, Miss, I am Mrs. Prestwick, Lauranne Prestwick. And they told me about you. I came to beg your help." And she looked at Adrienne expectantly.

Adrienne motioned her to a chair. "What is the trouble, Mrs. Prestwick?"

The girl perched uneasily on the edge of the velvet chair, but told her story readily enough. It seemed that her cottage leaked badly, raining in on her little girl Giselle and the boy Robert. She had begged for help, her husband had been desperately ill and had not recovered. "If only you could persuade my lord to do something!"

Adrienne started to say, "If you would but speak to my lord yourself, I am sure he will——"

"No, no, he will not! But he will do anything for you, my lady!" said the girl earnestly. Her red, work-roughened hands clasped each other in her lap.

"I will ask him," Adrienne promised slowly, with a sigh.

At dinner that evening, she brought up the subject, to be met by a hard glare, and a curt refusal. "The man is lazy, not sick. His family has refused to do what I wish. Let them fix their own roof. I do not give charity!"

"If we could but go—and see—if the situation is as she said," Adrienne pleaded, her hand reaching out timidly to touch his big hand. It turned on the table, his fingers grasped hers tightly. He scowled down at her.

But the next day, he curtly told her they were driving out. And the carriage was directed to the small cottage of the Prestwick family. Lauranne Prestwick ran out to meet them, her face glowing with excitement. Behind her came the loveliest little girl Adrienne had ever seen. The small child gazed and gazed at her, with wide blue eyes, her fairy face enchanting.

"This is my little Giselle," Lauranne introduced the child. The little one put her hand into Adrienne's outstretched hand, and gave her a small elfin smile. Adrienne's heart was caught at once, and she held the child's hand as they were conducted into the cottage to inspect the leaking roof and the damage done.

A man lay on a bed in one small bedroom. He made a feeble effort to rise. His cheeks were flushed red, his eyes bright and strange. Vincent looked at him, and frowned. "I'll have the doctor sent for," he said, curtly. "How long have you been like this?"

The man could not reply. His wife said, "Three weeks, my lord. And no cooling of the fever."

Giselle's small hand pressed Adrienne's. Adrienne squeezed it in reply. "I walk on the moors," whispered the girl, in the tone of one confiding a secret. "I pick flowers and bring them home to my papa."

"That is lovely, dear," whispered Adrienne, and kissed the pretty little cheek. She looked up to see Vincent scowling down at them both, but she had the odd feeling he was not angry.

"I'll send a man to fix the roof for you. Stay in bed until the doctor allows you to rise. And another man shall come to do your chores, until you can do them again." And Vincent marched out, impatiently, as though he were furious with them all.

In the carriage on the way home, Vincent put his arm about Adrienne again. She thought he would renew his wild threats and force her to accept him in marriage.

Instead, his voice was quiet. "Adrienne, did you like that little girl?"

"Oh, yes," she replied, relieved. "Oh, Vincent, she was adorable! Such a little angel!"

"Yes, I thought so." He hesitated, then went on, very gently, "Should you not like one of those little angels for your own, my dear?"

She glanced up at him, flushing a wild rose color, her blue eyes surprised. "Oh—I—I had not—thought—"

His finger touched her cheek very gently, he smiled down at her tenderly. "You bring out the good in me I had not thought was there, my little angel. Will you not marry me, and help me? And in return, I shall see to it that you have a little angel for your own. Or a boy, perhaps. Should you like a boy, as wild as your wild husband?"

His eyes were teasing and mischievous, not angry and glaring. She pressed her flushed face to his chest. He would not accept a no. She had nowhere to go, he was so good to her, and perhaps—perhaps she was a good influence on him. She might be able to do good here with his tenants, if she married him.

"Will you say yes now?" he whispered into her ear.

She hesitated, then daringly said, into his waistcoat, "Yes! Yes, Vincent."

She thought he would be rough and dominating, passionate, scaring her, but instead, he held her gently and pressed his cheek to her blonde hair.

That evening, he was so kind and pleasant, that she was quite encouraged. He talked to her a long time, about the family of his mother and hers, about their future together, about wedding plans. She did not get frightened at all.

The next day, she began to regret her acceptance. He was going ahead on the wedding plans, studying which dress she would wear, and what veil, and how they might go away to London on their honeymoon. Or perhaps they would have their honeymoon quietly in the castle, and later on he would take her to London. He made it all seem so final!

She finally ran away from it all, by saying she would explore the castle a bit more. He went out to see to his horses, and she went to the East Wing, where there were some rooms she had not seen. He had said she might open up what rooms she wished, and she was curious to see what was there.

She explored one room after another, and thought the castle a very rabbit warran with its many corridors and suites. She finally came to one grand suite of rooms at the far end of the East Wing, and found the windows overlooked the lake and the pretty fantasy.

She was standing at the windows, musing, when she felt someone behind her. Was it Vincent, or one of the maids? She turned, a little smile of welcome on her lips, to stare, transfixed.

A lady stood there, a lady looking much like herself. She was small and blonde, but with flashing green eyes like Vincent's.

"Adrienne—you are Adrienne," said the low charming

47

voice. The figure smiled, and advanced forward to meet her. Adrienne backed against the window, her eyes widening, her blood chilling in her veins. "Don't be frightened, my dear. I wanted to ask you to please—please, go ahead, and marry my son Vincent! He needs you so much. You will be good for him. My child? Don't be afraid—"

But Adrienne was afraid, desperately afraid. For the figure was utterly transparent. Through the white muslin dress and the smiling face and the blonde head she could see clearly outlined the sofa and wall behind her. It was a ghost. A beautiful blonde smiling ghost. The ghost of Vincent's mother.

"Who—who—why—" she stammered.

"Oh, you wonder about me?" said the low chiming tones. "You see—I did not receive a Christian burial. I have to wander the face of the earth! Oh—it is so lonely and so frightening, that often I come back here, and find comfort in the home I dearly loved. Oh, my dear, do marry my son, Vincent. There is good in him—and you are bringing it out. I have watched you—" And the lovely white hands were outstretched appealingly to Adrienne. The white figure moved closer to her.

With a choked cry, Adrienne sprang past her, avoiding the figure, and dashed out the door, and down the hall. She had to run, run, run, for the woman was a ghost! And she could not bear the terror of it.

CHAPTER 5

Adrienne ran down the stairs, almost falling in her haste. She caught at the railing, sobbed a little frightened cry, and tumbled down the rest of the stairs as fast as she could go.

The footman near the door stared at her in surprise, his young face concerned. "Miss?" he said, starting toward her.

"Where—where is—my lord?" she panted.

48

"He has gone to the jade study, miss. Let me escort you—"

But she dashed past him, around the stairwell, down the hall toward Vincent's study. She found the door open, Vincent seated at the huge black desk, frowning over some papers. He glanced up when she ran in, his green eyes alert.

He got up. She ran to him, sobbing, "Oh, Vincent—Vincent—"

His long arms closed about her firmly, comfortingly. "What is it? Who has dared to frighten you?" he asked, angrily.

"Oh—Vincent—" She was crying now, tears streaming down her cheeks. "I saw—I saw—a ghost—a blonde ghost—she said—she was—your mother—oh, Vincent, she scared me so much—oh, I am so frightened, I know I saw—"

She felt the change in him as he held her. A warmth seemed to come from him, a strange heat. He held her back a little from him, staring down into her face, into the misty blue eyes.

"Tell me exactly what you saw. What did she say to you?" His grip was hard on her waist.

She caught her breath, gathered her scattered thoughts, and told him what she had seen, and where. What the lady had said to her. "She said—she wanted me—to marry you—oh, Vincent, how could I have imagined such a thing? She seemed so real, I could see her blonde hair and green eyes, and her lovely smile—"

"You saw her," he said softly, triumphantly, his green eyes blazing. "You saw her! And she has refused to come to visit me! Yet she is here! Mother!" he said commandingly, looking past Adrienne at the empty doorway. "Mother, come and speak to me. Mother! I command you to appear."

Adrienne twisted her small head around, frightened. But no one came. Vincent laughed a little, oddly.

"She is so stubborn, so obstinate! She swore she would not come to me, and she has not. But she has come to you! Oh, my little one! You must marry me now, you are my link with the past. Mother has come to you, she will visit you again, and you shall tell me everything that she says to you! I shall give you messages for her, and perhaps one day she will forgive me and appear to me again!"

"B-b-but, Vincent, I could—not—I c-could n-not have

seen—a ghost—there is no such thing—" She began to protest, stammering, puzzled. "It was an illusion, a fantasy—"

He laughed aloud, his face shining. He pressed his mouth abruptly to hers, stilling her words. "Oh, little one," he said, when her mouth was hot and stinging and crushed, "you shall marry me, I swear by all I believe in! You shall marry me, and mother will come to you, and I shall have the world in my power! Everything in the world that I wish! My adored wife, my mother nearby, money, power, jewels—"

He frightened her as he spoke so violently, so commandingly, so awesomely. She trembled in his arms. He saw her fright, finally, and laughed a little, and relaxed, and soothed her. His face so darkly handsome was bent wooingly over hers. He smoothed her cheek with his warm lips, gently, not roughly.

"Are you troubled, darling? Do not be. I shall not let anyone or anything hurt you. You must trust me, and do what I wish, and all shall be well with you. You shall have everything in the world that you wish, I swear to you!"

"But—but I don't understand—everything—anything —" she whispered, and her voice quavered. He drew her close, and she put her cheek on his soft silk shirt. He frightened her with his strange moods, but when he was gentle with her, she wanted to melt right into his flesh, and become one with him. Did she love him? She did not know, she was so a part of him already.

Vincent rushed their plans ahead. She was fitted for a white wedding gown and veil by the housekeeper, and the gown was ready in three days. The veil hung down over Adrienne's soft loose blonde hair, down over her shoulders, to her waist, in a mist of white lace, so fine it might have been spun by spiders for a fairy queen. She told Vincent this, and he laughed oddly.

"So it was, my dear," he said, his cynical mouth twisting a little. "You are a fairy queen, and I ordered the spiders to spin their best."

"Oh, Vincent," she said, and laughed. They were drinking their after-dinner sherry in her favorite blue room, sitting side by side on a velvet sofa. She put her fingers daringly on his large hand, to have them promptly enveloped in his big fingers. "You love to tease me. Do you think I am still a child?"

"Yes, believing in fairy stories and fantasies. Little one,

I shall tell you stories that are the most marvelous and strange you have ever known! I shall tell you of demons and mermaids, of devils and witches and goblins and ghosts, of fairies and strange beings of light and darkness. I shall tell you about living under the sea, and above the highest mountains, and what is more, you shall go there with me, and see the most beautiful places in and out of this world that you can imagine! No, they shall be lovely beyond your most vivid imagination!"

She opened her blue eyes wide at him, and he laughed softly, and pressed his lips to her cheek. He was gentle with her this evening, teasing her, and she liked him when he was like this.

"Oh, Vincent, just so your stories do not frighten me," she said, simply. "I am not sure I want to know about ghosts and demons and devils. I would be terrified, I am sure, though I know they are not true."

"But they are true, my love," he said, and laughed an odd ringing laugh. His eyes were beginning to burn green fire. She gazed back at him, troubled, her fingers twined tightly with his. The large blue sapphire he had given her seemed to burn on her left hand. "Forget it for now. Let me tell you the story of your ring. You see, I flew to a country far far from here, a country named Brazil, and I flew over mountains and valleys, until I saw some blue fire shining in the ground. I dipped down, and down, until I saw where the blue fire was coming from—"

She listened, fascinated, ready to laugh at his teasing, as he told her the fantastic story, of how he had found the sapphire for her ring.

When he had ended the story, she pressed her cheek lightly to his upper arm as they sat together. "Vincent, sometimes I don't know if your stories are real or not, but I do know that one is not real! I do love to hear pretty stories, though."

He stroked her upper arm lightly with his fingers, sending a strange thrill down her whole body. "You do not know what stories are real or what stories are not, my dearest! What is reality? What is truth? What is falsehood? What is fantasy and when is it not fantasy? Who can tell?"

"I don't know," she said dreamily. He laughed in her ear, and kissed the little lobe, nipping it with his lips.

"Ooohhh, Vincent, that tickled!"

"Did it?" he said, and did it again. "Do you not feel anything more than a tickling?"

"Oh—I feel—I feel—" But she fell silent. She did not know how to explain how she felt, a strange thrilling down her body, a little shiver of anticipation, an awakening of something she did not understand.

Her wedding day came abruptly. Vincent informed her casually one evening that they would be married the next day.

"To-morrow?" she gasped, her eyes huge. "But—but the priest—the chapel—or a church—and flowers—oh, Vincent, how can things be ready? What shall I do?"

"You shall do nothing but obey me," he said, curtly, frowning slightly. "The priest I have chosen will be there. The ceremony will be in the crypt of the castle. There will be flowers, and attendants, I promise you. Think of nothing but the fact that you are marrying me, and are promising to love and obey me forever, past death, into eternity!"

"B-b-but, Vincent—" she said, faintly. He lifted her wine glass and pressed it into her hands, and smiled down at her.

"Trust me," he said, and it was an order.

The next morning, the housekeeper came in with her maid. The housekeeper wore a splendid black satin dress, which rustled when she walked. She seemed in a high state of excitement. She helped Rosa with the lovely white dress. They bathed and dressed Adrienne in the gown. She had had no tea or food, she felt too excited to eat, but she thought it odd that they offered her nothing.

When she was ready, standing in the living room of her suite, Vincent came in. She gazed at him. He was splendidly arrayed, she thought, proudly. He wore a ruby red velvet suit, with his huge rubies on his hands and at his chest. His black hair and pointed beard seemed darker than ever, his face was glowing with excitement.

He carried in his hand a gold goblet, huge, with something red in it. Wine? she thought it was wine.

"You are ready, my dearest?" he said, fondly, gazing at her. "How lovely you look."

"All—except my veil," she said shyly. The maid was holding the shimmering soft folds in her hands.

"Yes, good. Now, first, we will drink a toast—to ourselves, and our future together. Come, my dear—"

"Oh—I do not want to drink wine—I have had no tea," she said, rather plaintively.

"Tea? On your wedding day? No, no," he said, and laughed, and put the goblet to her lips. "Drink, my dearest."

She tried to evade the cup, but he frowned, and persisted. She sipped, and almost choked over the fire. She had never had such strong wine. He took a sip of it, swallowed it, then made her drink again. It went right to her head, making her dizzy. She protested.

"Vincent—it makes me—feel funny—"

"A wedding is an ordeal for a bride," he said, gently, his green eyes glowing with a reddish fire. "Drink—you will be able to face it admirably with this." And he made her drink the rest of the wine. She swayed on her feet, and he put his arm about her, and nodded at the maid. She put the white veil over Adrienne's head, and the girl felt a sort of strange spell over herself at that moment. She felt in a mist of fog and fantasy, as though Vincent had woven magic for her with his voice again.

The wine heated her strangely. She felt hot all through her body. Her brain was blurred, so that she could not see straight or think.

She knew he was guiding her to the doorway. He held her firmly in his arm, as he took her down the stairs, and down again to the winding stairway leading to the crypts below the castle.

They wound down and down, and she held to the railing, and to some remnants of sanity. She wanted to protest, but she could not speak, her tongue was fuzzy and thick. Were all brides treated so, she wondered, puzzled. Did they have a good strong drink to get them through the ceremony?

She had never been to a wedding in her life. She had read of them in books, but none of the authors had spoken of drinking before the ceremony, that she could remember.

Vincent's arm was so tight about her, she would have fallen except for its support. They came to the crypt, and she wondered at the torches lit along the way. They passed the twin crypts of his father and his mother, she thought of the blonde ghost and shuddered.

She heard chanting. The wedding ceremony? They walked on and on through the rooms, one huge stone room after another, until they came to a place which looked vaguely familiar. She gazed about, her gaze blurring, her eyes unable to focus well. Had she seen that black altar before? Had she seen something terrible going on at that altar? She could not remember. Only a dim remembrance of some horror remained to tantalize her.

Vincent led her up to the black altar. It seemed that the housekeeper, Mrs. Griffith, stood there, and next to her a man in a black cloak. The man was bending to the altar, his face hidden from Adrienne. Then he stood upright, and turned, and she saw the face was hidden by a black velvet mask, through which black eyes glittered. Not green eyes, but black glittering eyes. She stared back at him, her vision blurring again.

The man beckoned to them, and they came forward. She stumbled, and Vincent held her up strongly, pressed to his side. Through the misty white veil, she could scarcely see now. Everything was blurring, blurring.

They said some words, she said what she was ordered to say, faintly, her tongue stumbling over the vaguely familiar words. They seemed to be in a different order, something about the devil, and the Lord, and marriage, and obeying—and a small gold ring was fit firmly to her finger next to the sapphire ring.

The chanting rose and built to a wild exultant ringing. She swayed in Vincent's arms as he kissed her hard on her lips, and then turned her to face the altar again. Now the man in black beckoned to a girl in red, and Adrienne thought she had seen this before. He made the girl kneel to him, then he stripped off the red muslin gown, and lifted her high in his arms.

"No—no—" said Adrienne faintly. Vincent snapped his fingers. Mrs. Griffith held out a gold goblet to him, and he put it to his wife's lips. Adrienne drank, unable to refuse. Vincent drank, drained the goblet and handed it back. It was refilled, he gave it to Adrienne again. She drank, her head swimming, blurring, as the nude girl was lifted up and laid on the black altar.

It could not be happening—but it was. The priest chanted, the people were swaying, then they began to dance, wildly. Adrienne's veil was back, Vincent had lifted it back before he kissed her. She could see—yet not see. Her eyes were darkened, everything was misty, the swaying forms, the wild forms as the people began to dance around the altar. The nude girl lay quietly, and the priest bent to her, a knife in his hand. The knife descended, and

54

blood spurted. Red blood, spurting out from the white throat of the girl.

Vincent unexpectedly pulled Adrienne to him, and swung her around off her feet. She was dancing with him, to steps she did not know, wildly, whirling with him around and around the altar. He was laughing, exultantly, his dark face blazing with an unholy light. His eyes were not green, they were red with fire. The priest was yelling something, the people were laughing and singing.

And all were dancing, dancing, around and around in a frenzy, faster and faster. Vincent whirled her around and around, then away from the altar, away, into another room. The room beyond the altar—and she saw dimly, a huge canopied bed. It was covered with a red velvet cloth. The canopy came up to a diamond peak, and it was covered with scrolls of gold lace which were inscribed with strange writing and figures. All the red gold, all the blazing red—she felt quite faint and hot and sick.

The housekeeper had followed them. At least, it seemed to be her, and another woman. They chanted, and the black priest came, and Vincent laid her down on the bed. He stripped off her white veil, and flung it from her. He stripped off the white lace dress, and then her other garments. It seemed to her that the priest had a gold goblet in his hands, and he bent over her, and dipped his fingers in the goblet. They came out red. Was it blood? She gazed up at him dimly, too frightened, too numb to protest, much less to loose the scream that bubbled in her throat.

The priest drew lines over her breasts, red lines and muttered strange foreign words as he did so. Vincent was bending over her also, his eyes glittering bright red. He was watching as the priest drew red lines, dipping his fingers again and again into the goblet. The lines were drawn down over her breasts, down over her small round belly, to her thighs, down and around her thighs, down to her knees and back up again.

Then he nodded, and drew back. Vincent lay down with her, and abruptly, she felt a hard pain. She tautened, and moaned, wanting to scream, unable to scream. He was between her legs, moving hard, hurting her badly.

The curtains were falling about them, someone had dropped the canopy so that the walls of the canopy fell about the two of them on the red crimson velvet bed, and the walls were red velvet, streaming with the strange gold lettering, and scented with strong incense, perfume so strong it made her faint.

Vincent was lying on her, his weight hard and firm, crushing her under his hot body. She twisted her head back, the blonde hair loose on the velvet pillow, moaning in her pain and anguish. He was so strange and unfamiliar to her now, not the gentle teasing man she had come to like, but a hard fierce driving force that was hurting, hurting her.

When he finally lifted up and looked down at her, she was nearly unconscious. She was just aware, that his hands were more gentle on her, stroking over her breasts and thighs, that his lips were pressed more easily on her white shoulders, that he was trying to soothe her.

"It is all right, little angel, it is all right," he was whispering. "The worst is over, now you will enjoy it. Now you will enjoy my caresses. Press your lips to mine, love, respond to me—" And he put his hard mouth hotly on hers, and tried to make her reply.

She was too numb and hurt to do so. She lay passively, unable even to turn her aching head. She was dizzy, aching, bewildered, frightened, close to fainting.

"I command you to kiss me," he whispered, angrily, and his green eyes flashed.

She could not lift her arms to put them around his neck. He lifted one and then the other, and put them around him. He leaned closer, his eyes dominating her. His lips came close to hers, she could not respond or move.

"Kiss me!" he said. "Kiss me!"

She moved her lips slowly, they felt stiff and strange. He pressed his mouth to hers, and she was able weakly to respond for a moment.

He flung back his handsome arrogant head, and laughed aloud in triumph. "Yes, yes, you shall obey me!" he cried out. "You shall learn to obey me completely! You belong to me forever!"

And he leaned closer to her, and began to make the movements which had so hurt her before. She moaned weakly, and this time she did faint, as he gathered her close in his hard muscular arms. Her mind blotted out completely, and she fell back under him on the velvet bed.

CHAPTER 6

Time was a blur to Adrienne. It seemed she was back in her own creamy-colored room, in her own soft bed. She seemed to be lying there in a haze of pain and drowsiness.

Someone brought a cup of hot soup, and held it to her lips. A familiar masculine voice commanded her to drink it. She drank, and lay back, her eyes closed. She heard other voices speaking.

"The poor dear," murmured a woman's voice. "She took it hard, my lord."

"She will learn to enjoy it," said Vincent's crisp hard voice. He bent over her, touched her gently with his hands; she moaned and tried to turn from him. "Adrienne? Can you hear me? Speak to me."

She opened her lips, but no sounds came out. The mists drifted over her mind, and she fainted again.

He brought hot soup again, later, and she drank it. She did not know what she was doing. It seemed a terrible nightmare, and she kept seeing the black altar, the nude girl with blood spurting from her throat. Had it been the same girl as before? Had the same girl been murdered twice? Or had it been another girl? Or was she having horrible dreams that were not real? She could not sort things out, and her body ached, and her head was feverish.

Once she half-wakened, and seemed to be alone. She turned her head, moaned softly, opened her eyes. Beside the bed was a small velvet chair, and someone sitting there. She looked—and saw the small blonde-haired woman, the soft green eyes, the gentle smile. She stared at her, at the transparent figure in the chair. She could see clearly the outline of the ghost against the chair, with the back of the chair clearly visible behind her and through her.

"Adrienne, my little darling girl," murmured the voice. "You will be better soon, then I shall come and talk to you. Don't be frightened of me, I can help you. I want to help you. It is all so confusing for you."

"Yes—confusing," murmured Adrienne, and closed her eyes. She slept, and was not afraid, though the ghost sat there so patiently, and so near.

Finally she wakened, and was wide-awake, and alert. She saw the sunlight streaming through the long French windows, turning the creamy plump bedcover to gold. She looked wonderingly at her hand, it seemed so thin and pale, and it was an effort to lift it from the silken cover. On the left hand were two rings, the now-familiar sapphire blazing its blue fire, and a plain gold ring.

The wedding. She was married. Now she began to remember.

Something rustled near her. Mrs. Griffith was approaching the bed, on tiptoe, her face anxious. When she saw Adrienne's face, she began to smile, so kindly that Adrienne had to smile back at her.

"There, little lady, you are awake. Who am I?"

"Mrs.—Griffith," said Adrienne weakly.

"There, now, you're in your right mind again. My, you did have a fever for three days, dear! Rosa, send to my lord, and tell him my lady is awake in her right mind at last."

"Yes, ma'am," and Rosa sped away happily. Vincent soon returned with her, striding into the room, his face anxious.

He was wearing a handsome green velvet suit she had not seen before. It made his eyes seem even more dark green, his black hair jet, and his black pointed beard aggressively outthrust. He seated himself beside her on the bed, and leaned to take her left hand and study her face keenly.

"You are better, now, dearest," he said, positively. "You had a terrible fever. Do you remember anything?"

"Oh—I had—such a nightmare," she said weakly. "I—dreamed—that we—were married—only it was—in the crypt—and there was a—black mass—a nude girl on the altar—" Mrs. Griffith was tut-tutting in the background.

He shook his head, his eyes a little amused. "I must remember that you have a vivid imagination. I have told you too many tales of devils and witches, I fear! No more stories for you for a time, my dearest!" He pressed his fingers to the pulse in her wrist. "Much better, I think, though weak. We will have some more broth, Mrs.

Griffith, with sops in it. Tonight, some pieces of beef, and an egg stirred in broth. Tomorrow, she shall be much better."

He sounded quite firm and sure of himself. She tried to protest, and tell him she had really seen things, he only shook his head.

"You were right about being married, we were married right enough by the priest," he said, calmly. "Mrs. Griffith was there, and the main household staff. But you were quite feverish, and finally became unconscious. I carried you upstairs here, and you have been out of your head ever since. I should not have insisted on an early marriage for you. You were still ill, though I did not realize it. Well—it is done, and we are married, and I shall take better care of you from now on!"

"How—many—days ago—were we married?" she asked weakly.

"Three days ago, darling," he said, and bent and kissed her cheek tenderly. "Rosa will bring you some broth, then you will sleep again. By evening, you will be much better."

"I wish—I could—tell—what is dream—and what is real," she sighed. "I thought—your mother came—some-time—and talked to me."

His eyes lit up eagerly. "What did she say?" he demanded. She told him, and he listened closely. "When she comes again, ask her to appear to me. Tell her I am sorry about our quarreling, and that I wish very much to speak to her directly."

Adrienne looked up at him wistfully. "Oh, Vincent, do you truly believe that I am seeing your mother?" she asked. "How can it be? If she is dead—"

He brushed her blonde hair back from her forehead. "You will just have to believe for now. Sometime I will explain it to you," he said. "There are some strange things on earth which I have seen. You do not have my wide experience with such matters, and it will shock you too much if I tell you all about them at once. Do you believe that?"

He seemed quite serious. She studied his face with wide intent blue eyes. He returned her gaze straightfor-wardly.

"Yes—yes, I do believe you know much that I do not," she said, and sighed a little. "I must have been brought up in a very—narrow—way, with little experience of the world."

He smoothed back her hair again, tenderly. "I do not regret that," he said simply. "I would not have you brought up otherwise. It is my privilege to teach you now, and I will teach you the way I wish, and tell you the things I want you to know. That pleases me. You shall learn rapidly, I think."

She was puzzled, and frowned a little. But she was too weary to sort out matters. Rosa brought the broth and sops, and Vincent fed them to her, as gently as a woman could have. When she had eaten, she asked childishly, for her porcelain egg.

"I would like to hold it, please," she said, sleepily. Vincent found the egg on her dresser and brought it to her with a little smile.

"Does the toy please you, little girl?" he teased.

"Yes—thank you, Vincent." She held the cool porcelain egg in her hand, studying the gold design on it with pleasure. She opened it, studied the little coach inside, closed it with a sigh of satisfaction, and cuddled it to her chin as she felt her eyes drooping.

"I must find you more toys," he said. "Only you will not long remain a child. I want a woman as my wife."

She was too sleepy to answer him, and did not know what she would have said anyway. She went to sleep.

When she wakened, it was late afternoon. Vincent was there, tickling her chin with a pink rose, and grinning down at her. She caught the rose in her hand, and looked at it.

"How pretty," she said. Suddenly she remembered something from her nightmare wedding. There had been masses of black and purple flowers set about the room, and more black flowers on the crimson and gold bed. She winced from the memory, her face shadowing.

She brushed her lips against the rose. The maid brought some hot tea, and some hot biscuits and honey, with small slivers of cold ham. She ate with some appetite for the first time since her illness.

Vincent remained, and talked to her idly, about the house, some remodeling he planned for one of the suites of rooms, a ball they might give for some friends from London. "You shall wear a golden dress with sapphires to match your eyes," he said.

She smiled a little. "Is that a fantasy, my lord?" she dared to tease him.

"No, no fantasy. We shall give a ball, and grand

60

ladies and lords shall come in carriages, and we shall open the castle for the first time in many many years. And they will all adore my beautiful wife, but I will allow you to dance only with those I choose," he said, with a flicker of jealousy.

"I have never been to a ball," she said, dreamily. "Oh, Vincent! I don't even know how to dance!"

He flicked her cheek with the pink rose in his hand. "Then, I shall teach you, my love. You shall dance with the best of them. You have a natural grace and sense of rhythm, you will not have trouble in learning. As soon as you are well enough, I will give you lessons."

"How lovely," she said. "Oh, Vincent, it does all seem like a dream. Except—except sometimes it is a nightmare."

He did not reply to that. Later her dinner was brought, and he came to eat it with her, and tease her into trying a little white wine again. At first, remembering the strong red wine of her wedding day, she did not want to try it, but he insisted gently. She tasted it, and found the light chilled wine pleasant to her taste, and not too strong.

She slept well that night. The next day she was able to sit up. The following day she came downstairs, and ate with Vincent in the huge dining room. He brought a cloak for her, and took her for a short stroll in the gardens, in the early sunny afternoon.

"You are practically well again," he said, with satisfaction.

"Oh, yes, I am quite strong again," she said. "How lovely are the black swans, Vincent. How long will they remain on the lake?"

"All through the winter," he said, and pointed. "See over there, under the bridge, near the boathouse? It is warm and comfortable there. They will keep their babies there, and in the spring you shall see many more black swans on the lake, tiny little chicks you will want to hold in your small hands."

She smiled with pleasure at the thought, and they strolled on through the gardens, past the gardeners uprooting the last of the fall bulbs, and planting the spring ones. In the spring, she thought, dreamily. Who knew what would happen by spring? She was married now, and she and Vincent—they might be having a child. She would be more settled and happy, better able to understand her husband. They paused at the fantasy, and went inside, and sat down on one of the red velvet sofas, and now when he took her in his arms and kissed her, she was able to rest against him and not fight him.

"There, my darling, you are more accustomed to my kisses," he whispered, and brushed his mouth tenderly over her cheek, down to her neck. "You will not fight me now."

"No, Vincent. I—I love you," she said, shyly.

She was rewarded for her confession by a swift hot kiss on her mouth. She put her arms about his neck, and held him tightly as he kissed her. Her body still shrank some-what from the heat of his, but she would learn to yield, she thought.

They had a leisurely dinner in the dining room that evening, a strange dish of seafood for an appetizer, with some white wine. Then beef and red wine, and mush-rooms and buttered vegetables. With the chocolate cake and rich whipped cream sauce, they had more wines. She felt quite dizzy when they were finished. He laughed at her gently as she clung to his arm. He supported her to her favorite blue living room, and settled her on a sofa.

"My dearest, you will have to learn to drink wines," he teased her. "I am very fond of them."

"I know, Vincent, but you will have to make my head less giddy," she said, breathlessly, sinking down with re-lief. She pressed her fingers to her forehead. "Oh, things are going around and around!"

"Lie down and sleep a bit," he said, and lifted her feet to help her stretch out on the blue velvet sofa. "I will bring you another toy and tell you about it after you have slept." His hand soothed her dizzy forehead, she closed her eyes and slept.

When she wakened, it seemed quite late. The candles had burned low in their silver candlesticks, the blue candles he preferred in this room. Vincent was sitting in a nearby chair, smoking one of his long pipes, and studying an object in his hand. When she stirred and sat up sleepi-ly, he looked up and gazed at her.

"Oh—I slept so long," she murmured.

He got up and came over to her. He put a small object in her hand. She studied it with growing delight and fasci-nation. It was a small statuette, of a little lady, all ivory and gold.

"Oh, tell me about it, Vincent," she begged.

"I am going to carry you up to bed, and tell you

there," he said. "For I have a feeling you are not going to stay awake very long!" He bent and picked her up easily, and carried her up the long winding stairs.

In her bedroom, he laid her down on the bed. The maid was not there. He had closed the door after him, with a kick of his heel. She sat up slowly, feeling a little uneasy and shy.

"I should call Rosa," she said.

"Why? I can undress you as easily as she can," he said coolly. He began to unbutton her dress, his large fingers deftly moving over the little buttons of her bodice. She was wearing a rose dress, of softest silk and lace. She watched his fingers moving, and began to wonder and worry.

"Were—you—going to tell me—about this little lady?" she asked, clutching the figurine like a talisman.

"In time," he said. He lifted the dress over her head, flung it over a chair, and began to unfasten her many petticoats. She gazed up at him, her wide eyes troubled and very blue. He did not look into her eyes, but concentrated on taking off her clothes.

He had her almost stripped naked, when she finally got courage to speak again. "My—nightgown—is over there," she said faintly, nodding at the froth of creamy lace on another chair.

"You won't need it tonight. I will keep you warm," he said, a gleam in his green eyes.

She swallowed convulsively. She did not know if she could bear it, to feel the pain she had felt even through the dizziness of her fevered wedding night.

"Vincent—Vincent—" she stammered. "Will you be—gentle with me? Will you wait—a little longer for me? You do—frighten me—a little—"

"I do not want to wait," he said, shortly, scowling, his dark pointed eyebrows peaked. "I have waited several days already."

"B-but, Vincent—it did—hurt—"

"You will learn to endure it, later to enjoy it," he said curtly.

She bit her lips, and lay back. He began to undress himself, after tucking her into the sheets and blankets. His hands had lingered burningly over her as he had tucked her inside.

"Vi-Vincent—would you—tell me—the story now?" she asked, to put off the hour of reckoning.

"Ah—yes. This little lady is a goddess from Ancient Greece," he said, stripping off his shirt. She gazed fascinated at the rippling muscular structure of his arms and his strong back. He was so large—so much bigger than she was. "She is called Aphrodite. She is the goddess of love. She rose from the sea, fully grown, in a seashell of loveliest mother of pearl, of shades of cream and rose and pink and green. Even as she rose, men desired her, and she yielded to them, this lovely goddess, and made them strong lovers and powerful. You shall hold her in your hand, and have the courage to respond to me," he said, and came to the bed, fully naked and powerful.

She closed her eyes, but even behind the lids she seemed to see again his hard muscular body, from the proud dark head, to the wide shoulders, the hard rippling muscles of his back, the narrow thighs so strong and tough, the long firm legs, the arched aristocratic feet.

He got into the bed, and immediately took her into his arms. Her body felt light and helpless next to his heat. He cradled her as though she were a child. She clung to the statue of the love goddess with both hands.

"Beg of her," said Vincent, in her nearest ear. His lips brushed the ear. "Beg of her—to make you as loving, as generous, as passionate as she is herself. Ask Aphrodite to make you a very love goddess like herself!" And his hand began stroking down over her small rounded breasts, down to her narrow waist, down to her small round hips. His big fingers moved teasingly to her thighs, parted her legs. He moved over her.

"Ask her," he repeated.

She could not.

He frowned, and bent to her, his powerful leanness beginning to move on her slimness. She was frightened, as his lips began to press heavily on her throat, her shoulders, on her soft breasts. He seemed to be crushing her. She stiffened, fighting him unconsciously, holding herself from him.

"Yield to me. Beg the goddess to make you passionate!" he ordered.

"I cannot—oh, Vincent—spare me!" she choked out. She released the little love goddess to try to press Vincent up and away from her. He forced himself down to her, and his body began to move on hers forcefully, hurting her. She cried out, and struggled; it was futile.

She was so weak, so fragile, so small, against his huge-

64

ness, his tremendous strength. She fought him for a long moment, crying out, pleading, but he was ruthless with her, scowling, forcing her to yield to him. And in the end she had to give in, and lie helpless while he thrust into her powerfully, and made her learn him in new ways.

She turned her head again and again on the pillow, her eyes closed, the blonde hair flying, as he made love to her with what seemed to the frightened girl a terrible force. He seemed to rip through her like a whirlwind, tearing her to pieces.

He took each white arm in turn, and put it around his neck. She clung helplessly, and felt the hard muscles rippling in his back as he pressed down on her. He groaned, and was savage in his finishing, and she felt the flesh tearing in her tender body. She began to weep, silently, the tears running down her cheeks, from her closed lids.

She was so small, did he not realize it? She could not take him like this, she thought. He was hurting her, hurting her so badly—he quite frightened her with his fierceness.

His lips were hot on her breasts, on her cheek, until he was finished, and finally lay back. He was breathing hard. He stretched his long lean body with satisfaction, sighing. She lay limply, wanting to hate him, but not able to.

She loved him, though he hurt her so badly. She reached out her small hand for the neglected love goddess, and clutched the small statuette in her hand. Oh, Aphrodite, she said to it, silently. Do help me, Aphrodite, if you can. I want to match his passion—but I cannot. Help me, help me, help me!

Her fingers smoothed over the tender coolness of the ivory statue, and it seemed to her that the little cryptic smile on the face of the goddess was answering her.

CHAPTER 7

Vincent was a very demanding lover and husband.
Adrienne felt rather stifled with him at first. She never
knew when he would come to her wherever she was, in
her rooms, or the blue living room, or in the fantasy, or
the garden, come up behind her and start grabbing her
and hugging her.

He seemed starved for her, for affection, for loving. He
demanded much attention, was abruptly jealous over little
trifles, then loving and thoughtful again.

In early December he received a message from London. He growled and grumbled and cursed. "This means
I must go up there for several days. Damn it to hell! I
don't want to go. You come with me, Adrienne!"

"Oh—if you—wish," she said, slowly, looking up at him
pleadingly. She did not feel very well. She wondered if
she was acquiring another touch of the fevers which had
not totally left her. Sometimes her head would spin, or
her stomach turn slowly upside down, or so it seemed.

"She is not well," said the housekeeper firmly, later,
"and that London with all its fevers—they been having a
time of it, my lord! You don't want our little lady exposed!"

He scowled, but agreed readily. Adrienne felt a great
relief when he had left, and she was alone to herself
again. She slept hard the first night, wakening only to
reach out and reassure herself that the long solid form of
her husband was not there about to reach for her.

She was somewhat ashamed of herself. He was so good
to her, so kind, showering her with gifts of jewelry,
trinkets, toys to amuse her, flowers of every kind and
description from the homely pinks she adored to the
exotic purple blooms he admired. He gave her every attention—too much, she thought. She was accustomed to a
quiet home, alone with her father, absorbed in his poetry
when he came home after a day of fishing.

She spent the first day in the fantasy, with paper and pens, writing some slow thoughtful verses which comforted her in their creation. She had brought some of the little carnation pinks with her, and set them in one of the elaborate silver vases, the smallest one she could find. She curled up on the scarlet velvet sofa, and giggled to herself. She felt like a ragged kitten in a throne room!

The next day went more slowly, and she felt restless.

Mrs. Griffith suggested, "Why don't you drive down to the village and visit the shops, my lady? I hear they have some new silks in from France."

"And some laces from Spain," said Rosa eagerly. "Some black laces in the finest scarves you ever saw!"

"The village?" Adrienne frowned a little. "Here it seems safe—but in the village—I thought perhaps Vincent did not want me to go to the village."

The housekeeper gave the maid a quick look. "Now, my lady, he never said not to go," she said gently. "He would only want you to be escorted. Rosa will go with you, or I shall."

"Just so you don't go alone on the moors," said Rosa, her eyes shining. "That's the danger. The girls who been murdered and raped—"

"Rosa," said Mrs. Griffith, very sharply, and the other woman blushed guiltily. "None of that! It is sufficient for my lady to know that it is not safe on the moors alone. She might become lost. The rocks all look alike after a time."

Adrienne shuddered. She remembered all too vividly the time on the moors, when she had wandered on in the mist and rain, stumbling, falling, to be rescued by her Lord Satan on his massive stallion. It still seemed like a nightmare.

She finally decided on a trip to the village. Rosa went with her in the carriage, drawn by two fine black stallions, and driven by a groom in the livery of Castle Caudill, ruby and black colors.

Rosa was chattering eagerly. Adrienne waited her opportunity, then casually asked the question she wanted to have answered.

"Rosa, what did you mean about the girls murdered on the moors?"

Rosa flushed up, then paled, glancing uneasily toward the moors over to their right, stretching in a vast meandering line of rocks and sand and sparse growth.

"Oh, my lady, I mustn't say."

"Yes, tell me. I ought to know of any dangers, should I not? My lord would want me to be careful," she said, knowing the strength of that argument.

Rosa bit her lips, then burst out, as though eager to gossip, "Oh, my lady. There be several girls did wander out on the moors these past several years. Then be found later, their bodies all ripped up and throats slit!"

Throats slit. Involuntarily Adrienne thought of the ceremony on the black altar. She huddled into her warm plaid cloak, glancing toward the ominous rocks on the moors.

"One at a time, they be," said the groom unexpectedly, not turning around on his seat on the box. "A girl would go out, maybe a young girl about ten or twelve, or maybe an older one, about sixteen or eighteen. And next day she be found on the moors, her body all raped and bloody bad, all ripped up like some demon he got at her." And he nodded his head sagely. "Some say there be devils about these parts."

"Nonsense," said Rosa sharply, and gave him a sharp rap on his back, which only made the sturdy man laugh. "Don't you be saying those things to my lady! My lord will be right furious with you. Mind now!"

And she settled back and would say no more. They arrived soon at the village, and Adrienne and Rosa got down to wander about the shops. They looked at the fresh pretty silks, and Adrienne chose one in a soft pink which she liked. They walked on to the lace shop, and she studied the beautiful black lace mantillas, and even tried one on her blonde hair, but decided against it. It was so black, and reminded her of something uneasy in her memory, something she could not touch with her conscious mind.

They walked on, looking curiously about. She noticed one shop of herbs, a small dirty shop, and paused at the window. A woman came out from the shop, grinning at her. Rosa grabbed Adrienne's wrist commandingly. "There, now, my lady, you don't want to stop hereabouts!" And she glared at the woman.

The woman was small, stooped, aged, toothless, her grey hair yellowed. She was leaning on a cane, and peered up at small Adrienne from unnaturally bright black eyes. "I can tell your future in your pretty face, my lady!" she said, and cackled a laugh. "I know the future, I have seen it in my pretty ball! You will come to know the devil, you will! Trouble on the moors, trouble on the moors! I have seen murder, and will see it again!"

Adrienne drew back shuddering. Rosa tried to hurry her away, muttering curses under her breath. The woman's voice followed them, as she shrilled after them.

"I see the future! Blood, blood, blood! A child shall die, a pretty girl shall die again! Blood on the moors, murder on the moors!"

Rosa led Adrienne to the carriage, helped her in with the aid of the groom. When they were settled and on their way, Adrienne shuddered again and again, and finally asked faintly, "Who was that dreadful creature?"

"Granny Dille," said Rosa briefly. "Tabitha Dille."

"A witch," said the groom. "She be a bloody witch!"

"Witch?" asked Adrienne, and drew back in her corner of the carriage. She did not speak on the way home, her mind occupied with horrors. So there was devilish work about here in this new home of hers. She had felt terror, known vaguely that devilish forces were at work. But now—the witch—and her prophecies—Adrienne shuddered again and again, and could not shake off her gloom.

After lunch, she went to her pretty blue living room, and tried to read some poetry. Again and again her mind wandered to the horrible witch, to the events which had occurred in the crypt, to her own strange nightmare of a wedding. What was reality, what was a dream? What was truth, what was lie? Vincent had been so good to her, could he be evil also? The ghost who had appeared to her, she seemed so sweet and gentle, but could she also work evil?

She rubbed her aching forehead, and wished that Vincent would return quickly. He would laugh off her fears, chide her gently, then divert her with his wildly fantastic stories about flying around the world, and seeing mermaids and goblins, and meeting the gods and goddesses of Ancient Greece! She half-smiled to herself, thinking of some of his absurd stories, and how they had amused her.

The footman came to her, one of the newer younger men, looking troubled. "My lady, the village priest is here, and he insists on seeing you about a matter."

She started up. "Oh—I do not want to meet him—" she began distressed. But the man was walking in behind the footman.

He wore the garb of a priest, and he had a gentle face, she thought. She flushed when she realized he had heard her words. He smiled at her, understandingly.

"My lady, I know you are not a Catholic. I am Father James Francis and I have come on behalf of some of your parishioners, and mine. Will you not hear me? I have heard of some good you have been able to accomplish in spite of my lord's temper! I was encouraged to believe you would help these good souls I have in my keeping."

She stammered, "Oh, s-sir, I c-cannot believe I can help—much—"

"You have helped already." He waved the footman away, graciously. He had an imperious manner, something like her husband's she thought in amusement. They had probably clashed often in the past, the priest and the lord of the manor.

The priest seated himself on the sofa, and she sat down in a blue velvet chair. He was a man in his fifties, she thought. His bare head was covered with mussed grey hair, windblown hair, as though he had walked a distance to come. His black eyes looked brooding, as though they had seen much sorrow.

"I will be frank with you, my lady. My lord and I have clashed often in the past, and he will no longer listen to me. But I have heard you were different, more like the lady who was his mother. I never had the privilege of knowing her. I came to this parish some ten years ago."

She inclined her head. "Some see a resemblance in us," she acknowledged. "My mother was her second cousin."

He looked thoughtfully at her. "So you were related to the lady here, not to the lord? Yes, I see. That is fine. You knew, of course, that Castle Caudill was a family property of Lady Guinevere Caudill, who married Roderick Stanton. Few know from whence my lord Roderick came. But Guinevere Caudill was heiress of a great fortune and of this castle and lands. He married her, and began to run the place as he wished, as was his right, of course. But Roderick Stanton—imagine my lord Vincent, my lady, and add some more cruelty and harshness of disposition, some almost devilish quality to him, and that was my lord Roderick."

Adrienne was listening in utmost fascination. This was the most she had learned of her husband's family since she had come.

Father James Francis was watching her alertly, his

black eyes keen and serious. "You have not known this, I believe," he said. "Well, my lord Roderick was a cruel man. He treated the tenants with harshness and unfairness. His son is little better, I regret to say. Did you know that last week he beat one of his tenants for laziness? Beat him until the blood streamed down his back?"

"Oh—no!" Adrienne put her hand to her lips. She felt half-faint. There had been one day when Vincent had returned with blood on his hands, and a violent cursing disposition which was not soothed until he had had a great deal of wine at dinner.

The priest was nodding. "And he is—a great deal too fond of the ladies," he said, in a lower tone. "He has the habit of calling on some tenants—of a younger more attractive appearance—in their husbands' absence—and— But I will say no more." He looked down at his hands folded on his lap. "He has a very—passionate—disposition," he said slowly. "You will have much to forgive him. But you will forgive him that, I believe, for you have a gentle understanding nature. It is—the other— which I think is unforgiveable. A crime—truly—"

Adrienne knew she ought to stop him from telling her these stories, but she was fascinated, even in her horror. She had to know the worst, she had to know.

"You must—go on. Tell me," she said, leaning forward, her wide blue eyes begging. "I must know—the worst. You have hinted—I have wondered— Tell me the truth! Oh, I must know the truth!"

He studied her with grave pitying eyes. Then he nodded, and leaned forward to speak to her. He said, in a whisper, "I believe your husband is possessed of a devil. No, more than that. I believe he *is* a devil. Oh, I know you will wonder at me. But I have seen much evil in the world, I believe there is a devil, there are many devils about, tempting us, doing their evil deeds." And his black eyes began to glow with a strange light. "I am here to foil their evil purposes! I must cut the evil from the souls of men and women! I must cleanse them, even with blood!" And he lifted his clenched right hand in a powerful gesture. She shuddered violently.

"But—how can—you say—Vincent—is a devil?" she asked piteously. "He has been so good—so kind to me!"

"For his own purposes!" said the priest, strongly, remorselessly. "The devil has charming ways for his own purposes! He saw you, wanted you, because you are like

71

his own mother, whom he desired in a lustful incestuous way! I am sorry, my lady, but this is the truth! You must face the truth. And there is more." His voice lowered.

She was almost fainting. The heat in the room seemed intense, a cruel heat which burned her. She could smell something strange, as some odd incense, or sulphur, she could not identify the scent.

"What—more?" she was impelled to ask.

He whispered again, his grey wild hair ruffled, his black eyes burning, leaning toward her, his thin face intent. "On the moors, my lady. Several times we have found them. A girl will wander out on the moors. The next day we organize a search. And the girl will be found —yes, she will be found! But her body stripped naked, and most foully ripped to pieces, by rape and by knives! Yes, the poor body covered with blood, the flesh torn as though by an immense animal! Murdered, on the moors! And not just once, my lady! This has happened five times in the past three years!"

"Oh—no—no—no," she moaned, and pressed her hand to her mouth. She felt so intensely sick, she wanted to vomit. But no physical vomiting could relieve the sickness now in her mind.

"My lord Vincent is a hard sadistic man! You will discover this, to your sorrow! He will murder, he will stop at nothing. Only you can help him! I will tell you how, if you will do it! You can help your parishioners, your tenants. Do good for us! Oh, my lady—"

"What is this? Why is the priest here?" cried Mrs. Griffith's outraged voice. She strode in, an avenging fury in black satin, and glared down at the crouched figure of the priest as he whispered to Adrienne. She took in the pale horror-stricken face of the girl, and became furious. "What have you said to my lady? How dare you come here? My lord has forbidden you the castle. Out! Out! Out!" And she seemed to sweep him up before her, and with the help of the footman he was swept out the door.

Adrienne heard him going, as though in a daze. She put her face in her hands, the nausea rising in her, her brain spinning. The smell of sulphur was strong in the room. The horrors in her mind were overwhelming her. Her husband, the man of whom she was half-afraid, her husband was a sadist, a devil? Oh, the terror of it, the horror — She began to sob, her small body twisting on the velvet chair.

"There now, little dear!" cried Mrs. Griffith. Black satin rustled as she got down on her knees beside Adrienne, and took her comfortingly in her big arms. "Pay no mind to that devilish man! He is all evil! Do not believe him!"

"He is—a priest—" sobbed the girl heartbrokenly. "He told me—such evil things—oh, dear God, what shall I do? What shall I do?"

"Do not believe him," said Mrs. Griffith, practically growling in her rage. Her big work-worn hand swept soothingly over Adrienne's long blonde hair. "Do not listen to him. Oh, my lord will be so angry that he came! He is making trouble between husband and wife, that is what he is doing! He hates my lord for opposing him! He told you lies to confuse you and make trouble between you and my lord. Do not heed him, my lady!"

She soothed Adrienne strongly, brought tea to warm her, told the footman angrily that he would lose his place for letting the priest in, sat with Adrienne long that night until she slept.

But Adrienne could not erase from her mind the memory of what the priest had said to her, that Vincent, her husband, was a devil—a devil who had murdered, and would murder again.

CHAPTER 8

Adrienne was afraid to venture outside the castle for the next couple days. She remained indoors, to Mrs. Griffith's deep concern.

The housekeeper kept muttering dark words about the terrible priest and the trouble he liked to cause. "Just wait till the master comes home," she would say. "Just wait! He'll be in a right rage, he will!"

Adrienne found herself longing for Vincent to return, to reassure her, to give her strength. She seemed to have so little will of her own anymore, she thought. She had already begun to lean on him so heavily, that she did not want to think for herself.

She was feeling especially nervous and unlike herself one afternoon, three days before they expected Vincent to return. She scolded herself, it did no good. Finally she took several of her "toys" with her, the porcelain egg, the little statuette of Aphrodite, a favorite piece of jade carved in the form of a fat laughing god, a strand of pink pearls, and a triangle of hand-carved wood with an intricate design on it. She set them on the small table near the blue sofa in her favorite living room. Then she lay down on the sofa, pulled a rug over her and with her arm curled under her head she lay on her side and looked at her toys.

Slowly she recounted to herself the stories that Vincent had told her about the objects. Her mind slowed, and soothed by the little toys, she finally fell asleep, and slept deeply.

It seemed no time at all until she wakened, but the room was darkened when she woke. The fireplace glowed with a fresh sparkling fire, the windows were darkened and the blue drapes drawn. And she heard voices. Sleepily, she moved, blinking, trying to remember where she was.

"Adrienne?" It was Vincent's deep voice. He came over to the couch, bringing the chill invigorating air of the outdoors with him. He had just shed his traveling cloak, and his dark suit was dusty, his face weary.

"Oh, Vincent!" It was a cry from the heart. Lying there, she held up her arms to him. "Oh, you are home! Oh, I missed you so much!"

His dark face suddenly glowed light with pleasure. His green eyes shone. He sat down beside her on the sofa, bent down and pressed his cool cheek to her warm sleepy face. "Darling, darling," he said, softly against her lips. "You missed me? Did you really miss me?"

"Oh, yes, so very much, darling!" She wound her arms tightly about his broad shoulders, hugged as much of him as she could hold, with a fierceness which surprised them both. She pressed her lips against his rough cool cheek. "Oh, you came back early, how good, how good!"

He stroked her hair back from her forehead, gazed down at her fondly. Sleep seemed to have relaxed her inhibitions, she thought. She wanted to hug him, to put her fingers on his lips and chin, to kiss him, to hold him tightly.

"This is a lovely welcome, darling," he said, with a smile. His face seemed to have relaxed his fierceness, he seemed tender and gentle in his touching of her. "I should go away again more often, if it would encourage such demonstrations! But I do not think I can bear to leave you again very soon."

His lips pressed lightly against her mouth, so gently, so lovingly, that she was able to respond shyly to him. Presently, he went up to his room to bathe and change for dinner. She rose with fresh happy spirit, and went to see that the wines were properly chilled for him, and a good dinner prepared.

At dinner, he was full of his trip to London, telling her stories, one after the other, of marvels he had seen, of art objects and paintings. He had more toys for her, he told her gleefully, and laughed when she clapped her hands childishly in delight.

But in the midst of their happy conversation, she suddenly remembered the priest and his accusations, and her face shadowed. Her spirits were abruptly dampened, and Vincent sensed it at once. He studied her face questioningly.

"And what have you been doing while I was gone, my love?" he asked.

"Oh—I—went to the village once with Rosa, and bought a length of French pink silk for a dress. And—and the priest called." She looked up at him with troubled eyes. "I want to—to talk to you about that, Vincent."

He frowned abruptly, his dark eyes flashing green fire. "He dared to come here?" he said, his tone deepening, ominously controlled. "He dared to call upon you? I have told him to stay away from me and mine! I will have to speak to him again!"

"I will—tell you later—what he said," she said, a little faintly, her hand shaking on the cloth. "I must—tell you."

His eyes studied her face keenly. He seemed to be reading her mind. She wondered rather uneasily if he could. He seemed uncanny in his ability to comprehend what she was thinking without her words.

"We will talk after dinner," he said, finally, as the footman bent to serve him.

While they finished dinner, she had time to reconsider her feelings on the matter. He would be furious with the priest if he knew what the priest had said to her. It would cause more bad feeling.

In her blue drawing room after dinner, Vincent drew her down to sit beside him. "I will give you some of the toys tomorrow," he said. "Tonight, we will just talk and become acquainted again. I feel as though I have been away a thousand years."

She leaned her head gratefully on his shoulder. He was truly so large and so strong and reassuring. She felt as though she could depend on him for anything, though he was a hard and sometimes unfeeling person, she thought.

"I did miss you so much. And I was—frightened a little, Vincent," she said. "The priest was talking about the tenants. He was concerned for them. I wish—I wish you would let me go with you more often and see to their needs. Would you let me?" She looked up at him anxiously.

"Yes, of course," he said, promptly, though his dark triangular brows drew into a slight frown. "I will not coddle them, though, I warn you, Adrienne! Everyone must work for what he gets."

She spoke of that a little, and allowed him to believe that was the full extent of her conversation with the priest. Later, she turned the conversation to another matter.

"In the village, Rosa and I met a witch. I mean, it was Granny Dille, Vincent."

"A very minor witch," he said, with a careless laugh and wave of his hand.

She opened her blue eyes at him. He grinned down at her mischievously.

"Her spells frequently don't work," he said, as though he thought that was humorous. "She is very careless with her herbs also. Have nothing to do with her, Adrienne. She means evil."

"While we were in the village," she said, carefully, pleating her chiffon rose skirts with a shaking hand, "I heard some things. I want—to ask you—about them. Please don't be angry, Vincent."

"I do not promise," he said, and his mouth set. "I am not going to forbid you to go anywhere, Adrienne. But I wish you would have a care to whom you speak and on what matters!"

"Yes, Vincent," she said, meekly, her head drooping. "But—please—I have to know something. Do you—have —supernatural powers?"

There was an odd silence in the room. Only the

crackling fire in the fireplace seemed to flare up more loudly. She turned to gaze up at her husband's face anxiously.

"Supernatural? That is a strange thing to ask, Adrienne," he said, finally. "Did the witch accuse me of anything?"

"No, no, she did not," she said, honestly, then hastened on before he could question her. "I have heard things, Vincent. There have been murders on the moors. Did you —know—have anything to do with—I mean—did you know in advance about them?"

"No, of course not," he said, harshly. "What a question! You must be still ill, Adrienne." And he put his large hand on her forehead. "It is warm," he said.

"I am not sick, please, I am not sick," she said, but she was feeling rather ill and exhausted with excitement and tension. She put her hand unconsciously on her stomach. He was watching her sharply. "Vincent, do you have— demonic—powers?"

"Demonic!" he said, sharply. He gave her a little shake. "What is this? Adrienne, who has been talking to you? Of course, I am a normal human being. Do you know any normal human being who has demonic powers?"

"I don't know," she said, simply, and tears sprang to her eyes. "I don't know at all, Vincent! Sometimes you do seem to have—and the things I saw in the crypt—those terrible things—"

"You are overwrought and still ill," he said firmly. "I am going to take you up to bed and see that you sleep well! Mrs. Griffith tells me you have had only fitful sleep since I left. Well, I shall see to it that your overworking imagination is lulled, and you shall sleep tonight! You need more rest, darling, and there will be no more toys for you and no rides, until you are much much better!"

She gave in to his much stronger will, and allowed herself to be swept off to bed. When Rosa had undressed her, and put her in a white lacy nightgown, and tucked her into bed, Vincent came to her bedroom. He too was in his nightclothes, and over them a magnificent black and gold robe. He carried a bottle and two shining champagne glasses.

Rosa bade them goodnight with a little smile. When she had left, Vincent set down the bottle on the bedside table, and took off his robe. He slid into bed beside her, leaving

77

the candles burning in the room. He tucked her pillows up so she could sit up.

He poured the chilled wine into two glasses, and gave her one. "To my darling wife, and may she have pleasant dreams with me beside her," he said, with a little wicked grin.

She smiled rather shyly, her lashes lowered to her flushed cheeks. She felt rather surprised at herself that she had dared to ask him such strange questions about his demonic powers. Of course he was strong, and daring, and imperious. But he was a human being, the lord of Castle Caudill, and her husband. Perhaps she was still feverish, as he had said.

She drank the champagne in little sips, while he drained his glass and poured more. He began to speak again of his trip to London, some amusing persons he had met, a grand ball he had attended.

"Next time I go, you shall go with me," he said. "We shall dress you in a fine gown—I think a white ball gown with diamonds sparkling on it—and a good set of diamonds in your hair and at your pretty throat. You shall be the darling of the ball, but only I shall dance with you. I should be too jealous otherwise!"

She giggled at him. The champagne was making her spirits rise. "And what about you, shall you dance only with me? Or will you be attracted to other ladies, Vincent? Surely you don't expect me to sit in a corner and watch while you dance with other ladies!"

He half-frowned, half-smiled, and poured more champagne into her glass. When the bottle was empty, she was pleasantly dizzy. He settled her pillows down further, but did not blow out the candles. When she lay down again, he lay down close beside her, and took her in his arms. This time, he was gentle and slow. His mouth teased at her face and throat, and the soft rounded swell of her breasts above the low-cut lace bodice.

He lifted her arms to put about his neck, and she remembered the empty days and nights without him, and hugged him frankly to her. He seemed immensely pleased with her response, and talked to her softly, praising her gentleness and her warmth. He stroked his hand over her upper arms, and pressed kisses to them. He took a long time to kiss and caress her, and lean over her, and by the time he was lifting her nightgown to her waist, she was ready for him, all soft and yielding.

He was slow and gentle. No hard cruel pain, no rough thrusting of his body, no heavy weight on her to crush her. He was so sweet she could scarcely believe it, and she settled herself comfortably beneath him with a happy sigh. He made love to her for a long time, moving slowly at first, waiting for her to respond to the motions before moving on to the next stage.

By the time he had come to his climax, she was moving and clutching at him, and crying out with pleasure. She felt a strange heaving something inside her, a flash of deep joy, a sensation so intense that it half-frightened her yet thrilled her.

And the next days and nights were like this. Vincent seemed to have changed somehow. He was gentler with her, waiting for her, teasing her with some humor when she was shy with him, but not growing angry with her. She grew more confident with him, and dared to express her thoughts and wishes. At the same time, she wanted to yield her will to his, and their nights grew infinitely sweet and exciting.

She was in her bedroom late one morning. They had lain awake a long time the night before while Vincent enjoyed her, and when he had left her in the morning he had admonished her to sleep again. So she had slept, and wakened, and slept again, until almost noon.

When she wakened, it was with the sensation of not being alone. This time when she turned her head sleepily, and saw the pretty blonde ghost sitting patiently in the chair near the bed, she was not startled.

"Good morning, Adrienne," said the woman with a pretty smile. Her green eyes, so like Vincent's, lit up with beauty. "You are not frightened of me today, are you? I do so want to talk to you and tell you about Vincent."

"I am not—used to you yet, ma'am," said Adrienne, sleepily. "But I love Vincent also. I do wish you would talk to me."

"Good!" said the lady Guinevere, and gave a happy little trill of laughter. "I have waited so patiently for this. Now, I can talk to you about my darling son. What would you like to know about him?"

Adrienne thought. She remembered the long scar on his face. "Ma'am, how did he get his scar? Would you tell me?"

"With pleasure! He was always a naughty fellow, always doing things he was forbidden to do! Such an obstinate boy, he was, yet he could wind his father and me about his fingers, he was so clever and so loving and so intelligent. Well! There was a mean horse in the stable, called Black Lightning. I had begged his father to be rid of him, I could feel trouble brewing. You see, Vincent had ridden every horse in the stable by the time he was eight! Yes, he was a born rider."

Adrienne was propped up on her elbow, listening with fascination to the pretty caressing voice, watching the display of feeling and animation on the lovely face, though it was transparent to the light. Behind it she could see plainly the design of the silk pattern on the chair. The blonde hair was like her own, though a slight grey streak went from the temple to the back of the head.

"What happened, ma'am? Surely Vincent did not try to ride the stallion!"

"Oh, yes, he did!" And the lovely face grimaced. "He took out Black Lightning one morning, very early. He and the horse were gone when his father went out to the stables. Roderick followed him, the grooms were too frightened for the boy not to admit what he had done. He had been gone two hours. He found Vincent on the moors, unconscious, the stallion grazing nearby. Blood was gushing down his face from a wide gash where he had fallen on a sharp rock!"

"Oh—no—no," whispered Adrienne, her eyes wide.

"Yes. Roderick carried him back, having shot Black Lightning. Yes, he shot him immediately. He adored Vincent, our only child. I screamed and went into a faint. The doctor was sent for, and when I had recovered, they had my boy bandaged, and cared for. Roderick waited a week until Vincent was much better, then he whipped him for disobedience, in spite of my pleas!" The ghost sighed and shook her head. "I tried to command him with love, his father with stern commands. Both of us failed. The boy would ever go his own way!"

"He is very willful," said Adrienne, moving to a more comfortable position, curled in the bed. "I thought—forgive me, ma'am—I thought he had been spoiled by you both."

The lady smiled, and began to speak, then lifted her head alertly. "Someone is coming," she whispered. "I will come back again!" And she faded away in the sunlight.

Rosa came in, bathed Adrienne and dressed her, chatting happily about the lovely day. She put Adrienne in a blue muslin dress, the color of her eyes, she said, and took the girl downstairs. Adrienne went back to Vincent's study, and found him there. She sat down in a chair opposite his desk, and said, looking at him thoughtfully,

"Vincent, I know how you got your scar."

He touched his cheek in a rather startled way. "How did I?"

"Black Lightning threw you on the moors," she said.

"He did not! No horse ever threw me! He was startled by a bolt of lightning which knocked me from the horse. I told father not to shoot him!"

Adrienne smiled at him mischievously. "Your mother said you were thrown," she said.

He jumped up and came around the desk to her, his face alight. "You have been talking to her! Come and tell me everything," he commanded, and drew her over to a couch. He sat with her on his lap, and drew out the whole story from her. "Next time you talk to her, beg her to come to me, Adrienne," he said, earnestly, when she was finished. "I wish so much to talk to her again."

"I will try, Vincent," she promised simply, and received a gentle kiss for her words.

When she talked to Vincent's mother the next day, she repeated his request. Lady Guinevere only shook her head, her face sad. "No, he knows why I will not. I made a vow," was all she would say. "Now, would you like to hear about Vincent when his father sent him away to school?" And she told her more stories which made Vincent all the more human and interesting to the new young bride.

She also gave her gentle advice, about handling Vincent, about the household staff and her duties, even homely details about having the unused silver polished twice a year. She spoke of the gardens, and reminded Adrienne to have fresh bulbs put in for the daffodils and crocus. She told Adrienne stories about the household treasures, and where they had come from, about guests who had visited there, about the black swans and where they had come from. Each day, she came, and their visits became longer and more intimate, until Adrienne finally felt she had a true new mother in the strange ghost of the little blonde lady.

CHAPTER 9

Adrienne was rather ill the next couple weeks. She did not feel sick all day, but in the mornings she was quite ill. Vincent was most concerned about her, and told her to remain in bed until she was better.

She felt uneasy about it, rather concerned. She did not feel feverish, but wondered if she had caught some disease she could not understand. By mid-afternoon, she felt good again, and by evening, she was lively. But by the following mornings, she was always ill once more.

She was so ill around Christmas time that Vincent forbade any celebrations. They spent the days and nights quietly in the castle. He did not invite any guests. She was relieved enough not to meet new people, she felt quite shy about that.

Later on, she told Vincent, she would be happy to be his hostess, and greet his guests.

"There is no hurry about this," he said, carelessly. "They can just wait to meet my bride. Besides, you are too lovely. The men will want to court you, and I should go mad with jealousy," and he laughed teasingly at her.

"Am I really lovely?" she asked wonderingly. Then she blushed, it sounded like she wanted flattery. "I mean— father said I was like mother, and he thought she was beautiful. But I don't know if I am or not."

"You are, darling, you are beautiful," he said positively, and brushed back her blonde hair lovingly. "I thought you were quite pretty when I first met you. But now you glow and shine and sparkle like the angel you are. I like to think I have something to do with this, that love makes you more beautiful," and he bent and kissed each closed eyelid.

He had left her then, and she lay back in bed with her eyes shut, thinking about him. He was so gentle and kind to her now. She had everything in the world. If only she did not feel quite so ill—

"Adrienne?" The soft voice made her open her eyes and smile. "Good morning, my daughter!" It was the ghost, sitting and smiling in the chair that Vincent had recently vacated.

"Oh, good morning, ma'am!"

"I wish you would call me mother," said the ghost rather plaintively.

"I should like that immensely—mother." Adrienne sat up slowly, and plumped pillows behind her. "Oooh—that made me feel funny," she said involuntarily, wincing. She put her hand to her mouth. "I have been a bit sick, mother."

The ghost did not seem distressed. Her green eyes twinkled at Adrienne. "So you have, my dear. You have been sick every morning. But don't worry, you will soon be over this phase of it. Then you will feel grand. I did myself, and you are very like me."

Adrienne opened her blue eyes wide at her. "Why? Did you have this disease also?" she asked innocently.

Lady Guinevere gave a little trill of laughter. "Oh, my dear, don't you know what is the matter with you? And my poor Vincent, he is really ignorant of ladies, though he thinks he is so sophisticated!"

"Oh—well, what is wrong with me?"

Lady Guinevere reached over and Adrienne felt a light chilly touch on her hand, a very cautious touch. She did not draw back, though this was the first time the ghost had touched her. She held her hand palm outward, and let the little slim fingers trail over her palm and fingers. "You are going to have a little baby, my dearest," said the lady, simply. "You are going to have Vincent's child."

"Oh! Oh! Is that it!" Adrienne stared at her, then began to smile. She drew a deep happy breath. "Is that what is wrong! Oh—will Vincent be pleased?"

"You must tell him and find out—oh, he is coming!" said the lady, and faded into sunlight.

Vincent strode in, frowning, from his bedroom next door. "I heard voices in here," he said, sharply, glancing about.

Adrienne gazed up at him. "Your mother was here, Vincent. And she told me—why I am sick."

He sat down on the edge of the bed, glancing about alertly. "Mother? Mother, come back!" he ordered. He shook his head in annoyance. "Mother! I order you to come! At once!"

There was complete silence, and no one appeared. He sighed, and bent to kiss Adrienne's forehead. "Now, tell me what she said, since she is so obstinate and stubborn and willful in not coming to me," he said, and glanced about hopefully.

Adrienne giggled at him. He hoped to provoke his mother into coming, but she thought his mother had every bit as firm a will as her son! "Your mother told me—" She paused and looked up at him shyly, anxiously. "I do hope you will be pleased, Vincent. She said—" She hesitated once again.

"Tell me, I shall not be angry with you, little one," he said, tenderly, brushing the backs of his fingers against her soft pink cheek. "What is it?"

"I am—we are—I am—going to have—a little baby," she said, rather breathlessly, ending in a rush. She studied his dark saturnine face questioningly.

"A baby?" he said, sounding stunned. He stared down at her, his dark green eyes wide. "A—baby? You? Already? But Adrienne—this is—this is glorious! You are going to have a child! That is why—the sickness in the morning. Oh, what a fool I was. I thought you had caught a fever!" His face lightened and began to glow.

He caught her hands in his, and squeezed them strongly. Her little fingers returned the pressure, the happiness beginning to spread through her. "Isn't it silly?" she said, simply. "I did not guess at all what was wrong with me. Now, I am so happy."

"Happy? You are? You want my child?" He questioned her so sharply that she was puzzled, and studied his face again.

"Oh, yes, Vincent. I do want your child, so very much. I do hope the first child will be a boy. I should like to give you a boy."

The glow in his face and in his eyes deepened, and became so radiant that she could scarcely bear to look at him, yet she could not look away. He bent and kissed her lips, so lightly, so tenderly and sweetly that tears sprang to her eyes. He took her gently in his arms, and kissed her, and whispered lovely things to her, so that she blushed and hid her face but did not want him to stop saying them.

The next few months, January, February, March, were glowingly happy ones for Adrienne and Vincent. He seemed to have discarded his arrogant harsh disposition, and was so gentle with her that she could scarcely believe he was the same person. Vincent seemed to have changed completely from the rough cursing man she had first seen in the innyard.

His mother came to her almost every morning, and talked to her, giving her advice and practical directions for care of herself. When the servants learned of the coming event, she was treated with more care than she had ever known in her life. They would scarcely let her take a step alone, or move, or lift an object. Someone was always there to do it for her.

The castle was peaceful as the months went on. The priest did not come, Adrienne did not care to ride down to the village. She did ride out with Vincent in the carriage on good days, warmly wrapped in a rug, with her cloak about her, on very short trips only.

The tenants came to look for her, and would come up to the carriage to talk to her, shyly at first, then with more seriousness and frankness as they realized her genuine interest in them. Vincent was sometimes sardonic about it, but he would leave her to talk to the women while he strode about the farms with the men. The children would climb up in the carriage with her, and sit at her feet or beside her as they talked.

One woman said to her bluntly, a young woman with three small ones of her own, "You are so different from what we thought the lord would marry. We thought he would marry one like himself, haughty and uncaring about us."

"Oh, he does care, he does," said Adrienne passionately, hoping it was quite true. "He has always worked hard, and he thinks everyone should work hard, that is all. Once he is convinced a person works hard, he will unbend and be gracious, I know it."

The woman smiled, a cynical twist to her mouth. "You are the good influence on him, my lady Adrienne," she said, simply. "If it were not for you, he would let us go to the dogs, I think."

"Oh, no, you are wrong. He is good and kind, I know this. He is only—hard sometimes, and arrogant, and does not always show his good nature to you," she said, anxiously.

"The priest says he is a devil," said the woman, slowly. And truly, we did think so until he married you. Now, he seems different. But the priest still speaks violently against him."

"The priest is wrong, he does not know my husband," said Adrienne, violently. "If he knew him truly, he would know he is a good man, he does good works!"

"Can a devil do good works? Can a good man do evil?" said the woman sharply, thoughtfully, with a frown. "I still wonder about—many things." She caught herself up as Vincent strode toward them, flinging crisp directions at the farmer with him. Her face went still, studying Vincent as he came, her eyes keen.

The baby in the woman's arms, nodding sleepily against her shoulder, caught Vincent's attention. He smiled at it, his face going suddenly tender. "Will the babe come to me?" he asked, unexpectedly. Before either could object, he took the tiny one into his hands and held it against him. He looked down at the sleepy face, the blinking eyelids, and smiled again. "Ah, the little wee one. We are expecting one ourselves," he said to the woman.

Her face softened. "Yes, we have heard of the event, my lord," she said. "May all go well, may the Lord bless your lady, and give you the son you wish," she added.

His face darkened strangely. He gave a last long look to the little one, and handed it back, nodding curtly to the woman. "I thank you—for your good wishes," he said. "Remind your good man to plow up the pasture early as I have directed. He will have better crops if the land is plowed twice this year."

"Yes, sir, I shall do it," said the woman, looking up at him wonderingly. He leaped into the carriage, flicked the whip at the horse, and they were off. Adrienne waved back at the woman, and received a wave and a smile.

Adrienne thought about the incident many times. She saw the woman again, and the woman was cautiously friendly, and always brought the babe out to see her in the carriage. But Adrienne kept thinking about her words, about what the priest had said.

Can a devil do good works? Can a good man do evil?

But most people were a mixture of both good and evil, thought Adrienne, unhappily. Human beings did both good and evil, and had to struggle through life attempting to live right and good lives. Was that what she meant?

Or was there some deeper more sinister meaning? Was her husband a devil? Did he have demonic powers? Or was he so clever that these simple people attributed supernatural powers to him, because he knew so much about crops and horses and farms and the weather and the moors and everything?

And who was the good man who did evil? Could it be the priest? He did not seem like any priest Adrienne had ever met, but her circle of acquaintances had been small. He spoke of evil, and she seemed to smell sulphur and brimstone. Perhaps he as a priest was more aware of evil than most folks. But was he under the power of the witch, Granny Dille? What was the link between them? Or did people make too much of that also?

She puzzled and puzzled about it, but could not comprehend very much of anything. She knew so little about human nature, she thought, to say nothing of supernatural nature. She was tempted to explore in Vincent's books, but he had forbidden her to do so. She had seen titles about devils and herbs and healing and more practical matters of farming. She wondered if the books would tell her what she wanted to know.

She sometimes thought she would ask the little ghost lady, Vincent's mother, but always something stopped her. She could not ask a mother if her son was a devil! She simply could not, it sounded absolutely insane.

Then one night in March, Vincent left her early, saying he wanted her to sleep soundly that night. He went to his own bedroom before midnight. She felt a little uneasy about it, he had been sleeping with her most of the times.

But she went back to sleep, happily, pressing her hand for comfort to the growing swell of her stomach, thinking of the coming child.

It would arrive about early September, she thought. By the time the summer had passed, and autumn was coming, she would have a darling little baby of her own. And Vincent was so happy about it, surely all would be well.

She slept soundly, only to waken with a jerk of panic. She sat up so suddenly she felt dizzy, and listened intently.

Chanting, she heard chanting, loud and triumphant, coming from a distance, but still clear to her! Chanting, chanting, like a church—only not like that. It sounded wild, demonic.

She could not stay in bed. She got up, caught up a warm wrap, and slid her feet into heelless slippers. She went to Vincent's room for comfort. She opened the door

—and stared at the wide bed. It was empty of him.

"Vincent!" she said aloud, as though she could summon him out of a void to her. "Oh, Vincent! I am frightened!"

There was no answer. Something called to her, insistently. Something was calling her—

She ran out of the room into the chilled hallway, and stood shivering. She could hear the chanting more loudly now. It was calling her, calling her.

She ran down the wide stairway, slipped, caught at the railing, and clung to it, panting. She knew this was madness. She should go back to her warm bed, and hide under the covers, and stuff them in her ears—

But she could not. She had to go. She had to learn, she had to discover what was down there, making that chilling sound—

She raced down the stairs, in spite of her heavy growing body. She went down the hall to the back, to the pantry stairs, down into the vaults, into the damp chilly crypts. The walls were hung now in scarlet, with more drapes than she had remembered. Flames of torches lit the way clearly to the far vaults. She followed the line of the scarlet-hung rooms, through one room after another, until she reached the large room with the black altar.

She was panting for breath, cold and scared, but she had to know. She had to know. She was not feverish, she was not ill. She was alert and awake, and this time she would learn the truth. She had to know the truth.

She paused in the doorway, startled, her eyes wide, her hands clutching the cold stone of the edge of the doorway. Her feet were cold on the stone floor. Scarlet drapes hung from the walls, scarlet trimmed with curlicues of gold in lettering bold and strange that she could not read. Black rugs covered the floor near the black altar. And standing there were people she recognized.

She saw Mrs. Griffith, in her rustling black satin, her face glowing with an unholy fire.

She saw Rosa, near her, her face uplifted to the priest in his black velvet robe.

She saw one of the younger housemaids, dressed in scarlet chiffon, sheer, her body showing clearly through the fabric.

She saw the butler, several of the footmen, some

88

grooms, many of the cooks and maids and valets and stablehands.

The servants were all gathered about the altar, waiting breathlessly for the ceremony. The priest half-turned, beckoned to the scarlet-clad housemaid. She came forward. He picked her up and laid her on the altar. The chanting rose to a frenzy.

She wanted to scream out, but she could not. She must see, see what they were doing.

The leader picked up his knife. He passed his hands over the scarlet chiffon of the dress, then ripped it from the girl, so she lay nude on the black altar, the scarlet chiffon dripping about her body. He passed his hands down over her body, again and again. He raised the knife, and slashed her throat.

Adrienne watched, her eyes strained and burning.

He took a gold cup, and held it to the girl's throat. The blood drained into the cup, then stopped its flow. He passed his hand over the wound, it stopped.

He lifted the cup high, chanting out words. And she knew that voice, though she had never heard it like that, high and shouting and passionate and demanding.

He chanted wildly, invoking spirits, she thought. And sulphur seemed to burn in the room, hurting her nostrils, choking her. The torches flickered wildly in the sulphuric fumes. The men and women began to dance about the altar, clasping hands, hugging each other, dancing on and on in a wild frenzy. The priest cried out his commands, and they obeyed at once, in an ecstasy of wild worship.

Slowly the gold cup was raised in the large black hands. The hands—black, she saw. Black hands, like claws. And they lifted the gold cup high over the girl, invoking the gods of his passion. Then he drew the cup down to his lips, and drank the blood of the young girl.

She pressed her hands to her mouth, trying not to cry out. Her eyes were burning from the fumes, she felt choked and sick. She stared and stared at the back of the head of the leader, the black arrogant head, the straight pose, the gestures, the commanding figure—

And then it turned. The leader turned. She saw the devilish glowing face, the dark saturnine face, the glowing green eyes flashing with red fire.

It was Vincent.

Vincent, her husband, leading the Satanic mass!

He stared at her, across the room, the glow of his eyes burning her hotly, burning her like fire.

She screamed out. It was like a torment, being on a rack. The fire, burning her— She screamed, and the merciful darkness of fainting flowed through her. She fell to the stone floor in a dead faint.

CHAPTER 10

When Adreinne came to, she was being carried in a rush up a long flight of stairs. She struggled back to consciousness, her brain fighting against a knowledge of what she had seen. But she began to remember, to remember, and began to cry out.

"Vincent—Vincent—" she moaned.

"Yes, yes, my darling, hush!" And he was carrying her up the wide stairway to the rooms above. His face was dark and scowling above her, the eyes flashing red fire, blazing down at her.

She turned her face to his shoulder, and smelled the flames and sulphur and blood. Blood. The blood of the young girl, that he had drunk!

She felt deathly sick and afraid. Afraid of Vincent.

Vincent carried her to her bedroom, and laid her down on the bed. Her hands and feet were icy cold. He took off her slippers, rubbed her feet with his hands. They were normal hands now, she saw, not black claws. Normal big strong hands. Big hands, which had lifted up a girl to the black altar, had slashed her throat, had lifted up a gold cup, had drunk blood from the cup.

"Vincent, Vincent," she moaned, and her blonde head turned back and forth restlessly on the pillows. He tucked the covers about her warmly, then sat down beside her. His black velvet cloak flowed about him, he was dressed strangely in a black tight suit from throat to feet.

"You should have waited for me to take you to a mass," he said curtly, angrily. "It would not have been such a shock. Were you so anxious to learn all?" He was glaring down at her.

"No, no. I could not believe it—I heard the chanting—oh, Vincent!" She felt faint and sick, but this time she could not feel any merciful blackness overcoming her, blurring time and horrible knowledge. "Vincent, you are—a devil. You are."

He scowled. "Half-devil," he said curtly, finally. "My mother was a human, you know that. But my father is a devil, Roderick Stanton. He comes here at times. He married us."

He flung the words at her brutally. She closed her eyes, opened them again to stare up at his hard face. "He—married us? Your father, a devil? We were not—married—in the church?"

"In the church!" He flung back his head and laughed, his mouth wide and curved like a sensuous faun. "Not for a devil's marriage!"

"Then—you are—you are a—devil!"

"Yes, yes, I am," he said. "And you, my dear, are married to a devil, and shall become my fitting mate! One night you shall participate in the black rites with me, and be initiated properly. You shall come to enjoy your new powers. I shall teach you much, my little one!"

She stared up at him in growing horror, in incredulous terror. "No—never—" she whispered. "Vincent—never! Not the black mass. Not the Satanic rites—"

"Yes," he said, positively. "You love me, you shall do as I command!"

She pressed her hand to her stomach. "And the—babe—" she said slowly. "The child—of a devil—oh, my dear God—"

He moved sharply, scowling. "Do not say that word again in this castle!" he commanded sharply. "I will have nothing of that here! I rule here! The devil rules, and we shall have all power and all command here!"

She felt very sick, but she had to match his will. It was a matter of evil and good, of life and death forever. "No, Vincent, the devil does not rule here. God rules," she said, very firmly. "I shall never—partake of the black mass! I shall leave you first—or die."

Faint though she was, she met his gaze steadily. And he crumpled. She saw the arrogance fade, the uncertainty that replaced it. She saw the red flame die from the green eyes. He took her hand, and his hand was cold and shaking.

"Not die, no, my Adrienne! No, you must not leave me, you must not die! I could not bear it!" He flung himself over her, pressed his mouth frantically to her silent mouth, her unanswering lips. "You cannot leave me. I love you, I love you! More than my life, more than my powers, I love you!"

She could not move, she felt stifled, weary. The smell of sulphur and incense lingered about him. She even tasted blood on his lips, the blood of the innocent. She shuddered. He felt it, and drew back questioningly, his brow stormy.

"You shrink from me? Adrienne! You must love me!"

"I do not know—what to think," she said, with a weary sigh. "I thought—I loved you. But I loved—what I thought you were—a strong fine man. Oh, Vincent, why did you not tell me this before? Before we were married?"

"Because I loved and wanted you from the first moment I saw you," he said fiercely. "I wanted you. I would take you by any lie, any expedient, any power I had! I thought I could make you love me by my force of love. And I have! You did come to love me, and want me. You told me so!"

"But you are—a devil. Not the man I thought you were," she told him gently. She longed to put her fingers over the suffering lines of his face, but she steeled herself, and lay limp even when he shook her by the shoulders.

"You must love me, you must!' " he cried. "Only your love means anything to me! You have made me love you as I never loved anyone or anything in the world!"

"Then give up your evil powers," she said swiftly, eagerly. "Give them up! You are half-human! Become wholly human! Stop the devil in you, suppress him. There is good in you, I know it! Let it be in command. Let the good rule!"

He stared down at her, then slowly shook his head. "No, I am a devil," he said. "I am a devil. I rejoice in my powers, which are stronger every year. You know the stories I told you, of flying here and there, of finding gems and treasures? They are true. I live in a world of fantasy which I have created, a world which I control. All about me are my servants. I rule in my world. I will not give up my powers!" And he flung back his arrogant dark head, his green eyes gleaming.

She closed her eyes against him. "Evil will not rule me," she said faintly, but clearly. "Good is my ruler. God is my guide."

"You will learn to change! I shall change you!" he cried out, with power and authority, so that she shuddered, and was afraid. "You will love and obey me! I will teach you, and you too shall become one of us!"

"Never. I die first," she said, and turned her head wearily on the pillow, and became still as death. She felt as though something, some bird of hope, had died in her.

He felt it too, by some subconscious link with her. He gave a great anguished cry, and snatched her up to him, holding her angrily against him. "No, no, you shall not leave me. Only love me, my darling, I need your love! It is the best thing in my life. I will not force you—but you must love me!"

She lay limply against him, faint with the smell of sulphur, the burning heat of his body. It would be so easy to slip out of this life, taking her babe with her, she thought. The babe. Child of a devil. Half devil itself. Oh, God, she thought, in anguish. Oh, God, she must die before she had a child of a devil.

He seemed to sense her mood, her anguish, her growing resolve. He clasped her tightly in his hard arms, and called upon her to return to him. He invoked gods she did not know. He cried out in a powerful voice to his gods of evil and underworld, and she was afraid, deathly afraid.

She still lay limply, until he had calmed himself, and held her more gently. He turned back her head, with his hand palming the back of her head. "My darling, my darling," he whispered. "Do not leave me, even in spirit!"

"I cannot stay now," she said, faintly. "You are—evil. A devil."

"No, no, do not leave me. I beg you to stay. Stay and love me. My darling, I will not force you to be evil. Stay and be my good angel, then. Stay and be my angel!" And he pressed his face to her soft throat, and she felt the tears burning his eyes.

She put her hand to his head, gently, then, pityingly. At her touch, he grew intensely still, holding her softly. She stroked her hand down over his head slowly. Yes, he was her husband, her Vincent, just the same, a naughty

93

wild boy, a wild headstrong man, a devil truly, but her Vincent. Her hand fell limply to her side.

He laid her down on the pillows, and drew the covers up about her. The mad passion and excitement had left his face, he seemed more calm. "Sleep now, little one," he said, gently. "In the morning, all will seem more clean and good for you. Shall I stay with you?"

She shook her head, and his face shadowed. But he left her, and went to his own room.

She could not sleep. She lay in the darkened room, and the thoughts went around and around in her brain, until she thought she would run mad. She tossed restlessly, unable to calm herself. It was too incredible.

Her husband was a self-admitted devil! His father, the man in the black velvet cloak she had seen in the hallway and at her wedding, was a devil, a full devil, and Vincent was the son of his father.

Her child would be part devil. She closed her eyes, and tears burned from behind the lids.

"Adrienne?" the gentle voice came.

She opened her eyes slowly. Through the mist of tears, she saw the dim figure of the shining ghost sitting in the chair.

"Oh—mother," she said, softly. "I needed you. Did you know this?"

The figure nodded its head slowly. "Yes, it was a shock to me also, my dearest. How I wept over my Roderick! And he was twice as hard and cruel as my Vincent. But he did change a little, I was able to change him a little."

"How did you, mother?"

"By love," she said, simply. "By love and by faith. You have a good influence over my boy. Use it. By good works, he will change. He must change."

"What can I do about this? He admits he is a devil. He enjoys his powers."

"By their works ye shall know them," quoted the lady softly. "Lead him to do good works. Even the devil can do good, and my Vincent and your Vincent is not all devil. His power has made him arrogant and hard. But you can influence him to do good, for the tenants, for the servants. For all about him. Encourage him, find good works for him to do, lead him gently along the right paths."

"What if he will not go?"

"Love him, love him, love him," whispered the ghost, and faded slowly away.

Adrienne sighed, and turned, and finally slept. She had nightmares, and cried out, and Vincent came to soothe her, concern in his face. He finally slept with her, and she lay in his arms, and felt some comfort in them.

In the morning, it all seemed like some bad nightmare the whole thing which had happened. Rosa brought her tea in bed, then she got up for breakfast. She went down to the drawing room, the favorite blue room, where Vincent was waiting for her.

He gave her a swift keen look, studying her face before looking away. She sat down at the dainty tea table, and the maid served their eggs and ham.

When the maid had left them, he said, "What have you decided, Adrienne?"

"I do not know what to think," she said simply. "Did it happen? Were you leading a black mass? Are you a devil?"

"Yes, all that. But I love you also, I need you. I beg you to love me and stay with me." Torment twisted his face. He no longer seemed so sure and hard and arrogant.

Maybe the ghost was right. She held out her hand to him, and he took it and clasped it strongly. "You will stay?" he said, anxiously.

"I must think, Vincent. I—talked to your mother last night."

His eyes flared up with hope and excitement. "Tell me about it," he urged, as he always did.

She told him what his mother had said and done. He nodded, listening intently.

"Then you will stay with me, and teach me some good," he said, and a little mocking smile played about his lips. His eyes had a sardonic gleam in them. Her heart sank. He would not be so easy to lead and to manage, she thought. Not easy at all. Very difficult, and he might also deceive her in order to keep her.

"I do not know. I must think of this," she finally said. She poured out tea for them, and thought how strange it was, that she was sitting here calmly pouring tea, and drinking it. And all the time her husband was a devil, she was expecting his child.

She was held in the power of evil, and she was sitting here, drinking tea! She felt a little hysterical, wanting to giggle and laugh and cry and weep with the hopelessness of it. She saw Vincent was studying her anxiously under his long black lashes, the green flickering as he watched her.

Did he love her enough to change himself for her? Would he allow her to influence him? Or was his power so great that she herself would become evil, become like the devil? She shuddered, and he brought her a shawl and placed it tenderly about her.

"My love must not be cold," he said, and there seemed a full significance behind his words. He bent and kissed her cheek possessively.

He would protect her—from others. He would cherish her—for his own purposes. He would warm her and hold her, to keep her for evil designs. The devil was here, and she knew it, and he knew it. He was the devil—and her husband.

She was restless and unhappy. After breakfast, she conceived the idea of walking in the gardens. Perhaps the lovely growing plants of April, the budding trees about to flower would soothe her. Vincent promptly agreed—and came with her. He wore his black velvet cloak, and it reminded her at once of the black mass. She wondered if he did it deliberately.

The black swans were out on the waters. He called to them, and some came, nudging gently at their babies, balls of fur just swimming uncertainly. They knelt at the edge of the lake and looked at the small ones, and their proud anxious swan mothers.

"The lake is warmer now for the wee ones," he said, and then looked down at her with a smile. "When our wee one comes, we shall be even more anxious and proud and careful, shall we not, my love?"

She nodded, her heart full of fear and wonder. They got up, and walked slowly under the budding trees. He held her arm so carefully so that she would not trip. When the wind turned cooler, he took her inside at once, so she would not be chilled.

She was torn, bitterly torn. Should she leave him, could she possibly leave him, when he was so tender and gentle with her? Yet he was a devil. In a moment he could turn hard and brutal, as he once was with her. What horrors would lie ahead for her, and for her child, if she stayed with him?

She talked several times to his mother about this, asking her advice. Lady Guinevere was troubled for her.

"My darling, I cannot see the future," she said, tenderly. "I do not have the gift. Mrs. Griffith is a witch. Do you want her to look into the future for you? She would if you ask her."

Adrienne shuddered and turned away. "No," she said, faintly. Mrs. Griffith, her good kind protective housekeeper, a witch. She could not endure it, she thought. But she must endure it.

Lady Guinevere went on speaking gently to her, soothing her. But still she could not make up her mind whether to stay or to go. And even if she did decide to go, where could she go? Where could she flee, that Vincent would not find her and force her to return?

Only into death, she finally realized. There was no escape from him—except in death.

CHAPTER 11

April flowered into May. The fruit trees budded gloriously and flowered along the lake, showering the waters with their pink and white petals. More and more often Adrienne sat beside the lake on a bench, or in the fantasy on chilly days, and tried to think.

Her mind went around and around, and she could not reach any conclusions. She could only wait to see what would happen.

She went out sometimes with Vincent in the carriage, driving with him to see the tenants. He was reluctant at first to let her go, growling that she was too soft-hearted. She would sit in the carriage, or sometimes descend a little awkwardly with her growing bulk, to walk with a tenant and talk with the women and children.

And slowly the tenants came to trust her and talk to her more frankly. They would tell her the problems that made their faces sullenly angry in front of Vincent.

"My lord said we would not have to pay the taxes

97

this year, but the tax administrator came and said we owed him," one tenant, a rough older farmer, blurted out to her. "He forgot to tell the tax collector. Or he deliberately did not!"

She went to Vincent with the problem, and he was angry. He straightened out the matter, and the money was returned to the tenant.

One of the biggest problems was the farming of land. The tenants were supposed to turn over part of the crops to Vincent, keep part for themselves. One woman finally confided in Adrienne.

"My lady Adrienne, it is impossible what he expects of us!" she cried out bitterly. "The land has grown poor. He demands the same crops as before, but with two pastures in weeds we cannot meet the demand without starving ourselves!"

Adrienne spoke to Vincent about it on the way home. He was furious. "They are lazy and soft," he raged. "If I allowed it, they would pay less and less every year."

"What about the pastures in weeds?" she asked. "Cannot you do something about that? Are the weeds the same as those damaging the animals' health?"

He scowled. "No, they are not." He shrugged uneasily, lifted the reins to motion the horses on again. He drove at a fast pace, until he suddenly realized he was jolting his wife. "I am sorry, darling!" He pulled the horses down again, and turned to her in real concern, putting his free arm about her. "Did I hurt you? Are you ill?"

She had her hand on her stomach. "I think—the baby moved, Vincent," she said, faintly. "Ooohh—I think it is all right, now."

"I am a thoughtless devil!" he said. She had to smile in spite of her wan spirits at his unconscious remark.

"A devil—but not thoughtless," she said mischievously, and her eyes twinkled up at him mockingly.

He kissed the tip of her nose. "All right now? I think you are, when those lights shine in your eyes!"

She pressed her cheek against his arm. Out here in the May sunlight, with the countryside flowering and greening about them, it was hard to think of the dark cold crypt with the torches flaring on red walls and black floors, and the black mass going on at the black altar. Perhaps, like the country, the good in him was not dead, it only slept in the cold, and when spring came it would bloom again, she thought hopefully.

"I will see about the pastures," he said presently.

The next time they went out, he made a point to look at the pastures. He scowled over them, tested the soil by feeling it with his fingers and tasting it a little. "It has gone salt," he said presently, puzzled.

"I do not understand, my lord," said the tenant, looking up at him anxiously.

"When has the salt of the sea covered this land?" asked Vincent.

The tenant and his wife stared at each other, he shaking his head slowly. Then she said, sharply, "The flood, three years ago! That was it, John. You remember, the water in the well was salty for a week!"

"The sea must have crept up under the land," said Vincent, frowning. "It has ruined the soil here for a time. Well, we shall have to treat it, take out the salt with washing the soil." He explained in great detail how to do it, but the work was beyond the comprehension of the tenant.

Vincent frowned, and his hard mouth showed his impatience. Adrienne touched his arm gently. "Could you— direct the work, Vincent?" she whispered. "They have not your knowledge of the soil, my dear."

His arm was hard and jerked under her touch. She knew he held in his impatient temper by a short rein. But he did hold it. "I can come on Tuesday, and we will begin the work," he finally said gruffly. "But you realize the land will not be fit to work for a year. You must not plough it up in that time."

He had to repeat his instructions and work with the tenants for some time, and he would come home and growl his anger at their stupidity. But he did work with them, and teach them to wash the soil.

The matter of the crop payments came up, and again Adrienne interceded. Gently she reminded her husband that the tenants would starve if they gave most of their crops to the castle for its maintenance.

"The quotas must be changed," she said firmly, anxiously watching his face as they sat in his study. He was sitting at his huge desk, frowning down at the papers before him.

"They have remained the same for twenty years!" he reminded her, an angry twist at his mouth. "Why should I be soft on them? If they cannot meet the quota they can leave, and I will replace them with tenants who will work harder!"

"They do work hard, most of them," she said, gently. "But Vincent, times have changed. And the flood three years ago did damage the soil. You need to give them time to improve the land. Meantime, they must live, and their children."

He scowled, and twisted in his chair, and gave her arguments why it should not be done. But gradually as they went out together and talked to tenants, and looked at the land, he seemed to soften his hard policy toward them. Reluctantly he allowed a few reforms on the land, made a few changes, then others.

Lady Guinevere came to her sometimes in the morning, as she lay on the sofa in the blue living room. She would sit with the sunlight streaming through her white body, and talk.

She said, one morning, "My darling girl, I am so pleased you have been able to soften Vincent toward the tenants. I never could influence Roderick. He would whip them also, though it made me weep. Oh, I know he believed they deserved it, but they have such a hard lot." And there were tears in her pretty green eyes, shaped like Vincent's, but not so hard in their gaze.

"It is a long struggle," said Adrienne, with a sigh. "My lady, Vincent wants me to attend a black mass with him soon. I am firm in my resolve not to do so. Did your husband try to force you to do so?"

"Yes, my dearest. And I was rash enough to give in once, which encouraged him to try to force me again. I was wrong, I thought to try to find out something about the black mass, to learn more, and urge him away from Satanic practices. I thought I was a strong woman, that my intelligence would win." She shivered, as though a little wind blew through her thin figure.

"What happened, mother?"

The little ghost patted her hand with its fragile cool fingers. "I was swept into the ceremony," she said, thoughtfully. "Evil is a strong force, my love, do not underestimate it. My brain seemed to have been taken over by Roderick's brain. He was jubilant at his power over me, he forced me to participate in rituals that made me shudder later."

"And did you go again?" asked Adrienne anxiously.

"Never again. I had thought to win Vincent away from his father. I failed. I was endangering myself when I went to the black mass. I almost died afterwards," she said,

100

simply. "I seemed to myself to have run mad. I tried to kill myself, but the good Lord stopped my hand. It was then I made a vow. I vowed that if I were not buried in the church, that if I came back as a ghost I should never visit Roderick or Vincent. They thought I was not strong enough to keep that vow."

"Did you die—then?" gasped Adrienne, clutching the little fingers as strongly as the bond between them would permit. It was like clutching a puff of whipped cream. She could just scarcely feel the little something in her fingers.

"No, not then. I lived, but I refused to participate in any black ceremonies. I tried to win Vincent away from them. Then three years later, I died of a fever. They would not bury me in the church, though I had requested it with my dying breath." She sighed deeply, and tears came again to her lovely green eyes.

"So—you have not visited them—"

"No, never. Roderick has been very angry with me," she said, simply, and a little mischief showed in her face. "He thought he could rule me as he did on earth. But he cannot. I can slip away from him when I feel he is coming toward me. Oh, he does get angry. He bellows after me like a wind!" And she giggled.

"And he did rule you on earth?" asked Adrienne. "How did he do that? By black powers?"

"No, darling, by the powers of love. I loved him long before I knew he was a devil. And when I discovered what he was, I loved him so deeply it did not matter enough to make me change." She sighed again.

"As I love Vincent," said Adrienne softly. "Oh, sometimes I do not know what to do! I love him so much—yet I am afraid of him and of his powers."

"Yes, and he is not so devilish as Roderick. My Vincent is softer and gentler, though he would be angry if I told him so! He admires his father greatly, and has studied under him. The son wishes to follow the father, yet he is half-human. My half. Love him, Adrienne, soften him further, in your subtle feminine ways. And as for your own child—do not let Vincent rule him completely. With your love, you will keep him human also."

"Oh, I hope so, I hope so."

With one of her quick changes of mood, Lady Guinevere began speaking of the castle and its upkeep. "Do not let the maids neglect the West wing, love! It is so very dusty. Have Mrs. Griffith to supervise them most closely. The rose tapestry has become quite threadbare, and other tapestries will fall apart if they are allowed to gather dust."

"Oh, I meant to ask you how to care for the tapestries," said Adrienne eagerly. "Does one beat them with twigs?"

They fell easily into domestic conversation, which delighted and satisfied them both. Unexpectedly, Vincent came in, and the ghost squealed and disappeared.

"Mother? I thought I heard your voice," he called sternly, with a firm note to his voice. "Come right back here! I know you are here, I feel it!" He glanced about hopefully, then looked down at Adrienne. "She was here, wasn't she?"

"Yes, Vincent," she said demurely, a little smile on her lips. Women did have their own powers, and they just might be stronger powers than those of the devil!

He sighed when his mother did not return, and came to sit beside Adrienne as she lay on the blue sofa. "Now, tell me what she said."

This time she did not confide all. "Oh, we discussed the best ways of cleaning the tapestries," she said, innocently, her eyes wide and fixed on his green ones.

Vincent stared at her. "You discussed—what?" he exploded.

"The best ways of cleaning the tapestries. And more dusting in the West wing," said Adrienne clearly.

Vincent raised his clenched fist up high. "Lucifer!" he yelled. "Lucifer! Lu—ci—fer!" He seemed to be invoking high gods. "I have begged my mother to come to me on matters of importance. Will she come? No, the stubborn female will not come. But she comes to you, freely, and you—you—you discuss how to clean tapestries! Lucifer!"

She started to giggle, then froze. A deep voice behind her said, "I am here, Vincent!"

Vincent looked up. "Hello, father!" The black-clad figure came slowly around the end of the couch and stared down at Adrienne.

"L-l-lucifer?" she whispered faintly, feeling very cold.

"No, only his devil," said the figure, in a hard tone. "I am called Roderick Stanton on earth. And you are the little chit who has Vincent around her fingers!"

She swallowed. Vincent moved toward her, and put his arm about her. "Don't frighten her, father," he said, quietly. "She is pregnant with my child. I will not have her frightened." He glared up at his father with a scowl which matched that on the face of the black-velvet cloaked figure.

"She was thinking that her powers as a female are equal to those of a devil!" said the father, seating himself on a chair near the sofa. She could smell sulphur, he was angry, and she was terrified. "Yes, chit, I can read your mind! It is quite clear to me. You must take her in hand, Vincent! Don't let her rule you as your mother tried to rule me."

"She did not do so badly with you, father," said Vincent, with a little devilish grin. "There were times—"

"Enough!" roared Roderick Stanton, his black eyes blazing fire at his son. "You will not defy me in my own house!"

"My house now, father. You left it to me, you recall."

The two figures defied each other silently for a long moment. Then each seemed to draw back slowly from the deadly encounter.

"Too like your mother," growled Roderick Stanton. "Well, my little chit—" and he returned to Adrienne.

"My name—is Adrienne," she said faintly. "I would be pleased if you would—use it, sir."

And her blue eyes gazed straight into the black eyes of the devil in black He stared at her, and his eyes widened, flared, and she felt the power in him as he tested his strength against hers. She stiffened, holding onto Vincent's hand, holding onto courage, her faith in God and in herself. His eyes finally flickered, and his gaze strayed back to his son's face.

"I would be pleased," she finally added, "if you will remain for dinner. If you eat dinner," she remembered to add, politely.

He unexpectedly bellowed with laughter. "You have courage!" he said. "Yes, courage! And I shall be pleased to remain for dinner. Only, Vincent, serve the port after the meal! I detest those light French wines!"

"For you, father, the port," said Vincent, and his arm hugged Adrienne almost painfully tight for a moment, before he gentled.

It was a strange meal, a delightful meal. Roderick Stanton sat in his black velvet at Adrienne's right, and talked of his many adventures. He had flown to Latin America recently, he told them, and was conversant of several new developments there, some revolutions, some discoveries of emeralds. "I shall bring you some emeralds next time I come," he said kindly to Adrienne.

"Thank you, sir," she said, quite calmly, and motioned to the quiet footman to serve the roast beef course.

Vincent sent her a little grin of admiration, that she could sit and talk so calmly to a devil, and listen to his adventures. But she truly found them fascinating.

In the drawing room, he lingered to talk a while longer, softening a little at their frank interest in his speech. "Well, I have not enjoyed myself for a long time like this," he said, finally. "Adrienne, I think you are a little witch, you are enchanting me with your wide blue eyes. I have not talked so much for many years, not since your mother died, Vincent! She did always like to hear of my voyages about the universe. It was the one time we did not quarrel, when we spoke of this," and he sounded wistful.

"You must return again, and talk with us," said Adrienne cordially, gently. "This is your home, truly, my lord! Feel free to visit us as you will."

He touched her hand gently as he rose to go. She found the touch hot, but not burning. "Let me give you a little toy, I think you are fond of toys," he said, and produced a small object from his pocket. He handed it to her, with a slight smile, his black eyes gentle at last.

She received it with a little cry of delight. It was a small gold-trimmed scent bottle, of the palest color, with a delightful strange scent in it. She sniffed at it, questioned him with her raised eyebrows.

"The bottle is amber, trimmed in gold," he said. "The scent is rose petals and ambergris, with a little touch of wild flowers from a garden in the Orient."

"Oh, it is so lovely, so lovely, thank you very much!" And she held it in her hand and pressed it to her pink cheek.

"No wonder she has you around her fingers, Vincent. Farewell!" And the black figure made a sudden fierce gesture, with both his hands and his wrists, and was gone, as suddenly as he had appeared the few hours before.

Adrienne clutched the little scent bottle, and wondered if she had been dreaming. Vincent sat down beside her, and kissed her cheek. "I am most pleased, love," he said, gently. "You gave my father a delightful evening, and I think he will return again. He does get lonely wandering the earth, especially since mother will not wander with him, or even see him. He misses her dreadfully, you know."

And he gave her a long look. She knew he wanted her to promise to try to get his mother to relent, but she would not promise. But she knew how they all felt. If she should die, she thought, soberly, she could not resist coming back to see and talk to Vincent, and touch him, and hold him, dead though she was. She would not be able to leave him entirely. But she did not tell him this.

She pressed her cheek to his, and whispered, "I love you—so very much—darling—so very very much—"

And he held her tenderly, and kissed her, and whispered words which even now could make her blush.

CHAPTER 12

May turned to June, and the flowers bloomed in the huge gardens of Castle Caudill. Even the moors seemed to blossom in strange flowers. The black swans swam freely on the lake, and Adrienne watched them by the hour, dreaming her motherly dreams.

She expected the babe in September, and her thoughts turned more and more frequently to the coming child. Would it be a girl or boy? More important, would it be of the devil or of a human nature—or somewhere in between? What could she do to influence the child? How could she win the heart of the child, and soften Vincent at the same time, so that he would allow the child to be good and fine?

Vincent asked her more and more urgently to join him in black masses. He now held out the enticement that her joining could help ensure the safety of the coming child. The gods of the black mass and the Satanic rites were all-powerful, he said, and they would ensure her safety and the child's.

She refused, though she was tempted to give in and agree. Her thoughts turned longingly to the church in the village, though it was Catholic and not Protestant. She longed to invoke churchly aid, but felt she must be satisfied with her own prayers and requests for aid. She did not fully trust the priest. Neither priest nor devil, she thought with a deep sigh.

June became July, and she grew heavier. She was so large that Lady Guinevere said she thought it must be a boy, and a big fellow. The kindly ghost urged her to rest often in the afternoons, and take long slow walks several times a day. So she walked through the gardens, and around the lake, and sometimes Vincent joined her, holding her arm gently.

He was so anxious about her and so sweet to her, that her heart was almost at peace. He could be so good and so kind, and he did love her.

Then one afternoon as she rested on the sofa, she heard Rosa whispering to the footman. She opened her eyes, moved a little, roused from her little sleep.

She caught only a few words at first. ". . . on the moors . . . last night . . . found this morning . . . body all ripped up, poor dear—"

"Rosa!" she called sharply, sitting up.

There was an abrupt silence. Then Rosa, her face flushed and guilty, came into the room. "Yes, my lady?"

"Rosa, what were you saying?"

"Oh, nothing, my lady, just talking to James, here!"

"Come in," said Adrienne, firmly. She beckoned to the maid. "What happened on the moors?"

"I—I have been—forbidden to tell you—my lady!" Rosa went white, then red, and back again to white.

"I order you to tell me!"

"Oh, please, my lady! I don't want to tell you! It was so gruesome, so horrible! Don't—"

Adrienne gazed at her. "It was another murder, wasn't it, Rosa? Who was murdered?"

Rosa twisted her hands in her black apron. "Flora Moberly, ma'am. It was little Flora, about twelve years old."

"The daughter of the baker," said Adrienne, flatly. The girl was a pretty blonde girl, with china blue eyes, and a doll-like obedience. She would wrap the loaves in a paper, and give an enchanting smile as she handed up the package.

"Yes, ma'am."

"Did she die on the moors?"

"Yes, ma'am."

"Horribly? The way—the others—raped and murdered?"

"Y-yes, ma'am."

"She went out last night? They found her today?"

"Yes, ma'am."

Adrienne leaned back with a sigh. "All right, Rosa. Order the carriage for me. I will go down to the village."

Rosa started. "Oh, no, ma'am. Mr. Vincent—my lord Vincent—he would be mad as fire!"

"He is not here now, Rosa. Do as I say."

Rosa protested weakly, but her will was not proof against Adrienne's. When the carriage was brought around, Adrienne went out wrapped in a cloak against the wind. The coachman and Rosa both had to help her climb into the carriage, so awkward was she.

She settled into the cushions with a deep sigh. She was not sure if she could climb down again, she thought ruefully. After her little one was born, she was not sure if she would remember how to move gracefully anymore.

They drove down into the village. Adrienne was silent, and Rosa kept twisting the edges of her black scarf in her hands, knowing she had done something she should not have. She kept glancing uneasily at Adrienne, muttering darkly to herself. Adrienne knew by this time that Rosa was a minor witch, not so powerful as Mrs. Griffith. All the servants in the castle were part of the devil's crew, witches, warlocks, some devils.

"Where shall the driver go, ma'am?" Rosa finally asked, as the carriage went at a spanking pace into the main street. Adrienne looked from right to left. There was a darkness on the village in spite of the bright July sunlight. There were uneasy hard looks on faces, wildness in some eyes. Some of the shops were closed and barred, including the baker's, with a black wreath on the door.

"Just drive along slowly," said Adrienne finally, as the coachman glanced around and down at her. His eyes were troubled and uneasy also, she thought.

They drove slowly. No one greeted her, though many stared at her, and then away. She waited for some to come up to the carriage. Finally one woman, bolder than the others, looked full at her.

"Stop the carriage," said Adrienne, and beckoned to the woman. She came up slowly, her feet betraying her real nervousness.

"Good afternoon, Mrs. Fletcher," she said to the woman.

"Good afternoon, my lady," and the woman bobbed a quick curtsey, her eyes fixed on Adrienne's in wide curiosity.

"I have heard about the tragedy of Flora Moberly," said Adrienne, quietly. "Tell me what you know of it."

"Well, my lady." The woman put her hands on her hips, settling herself to gossip with eagerness, though the expression on her face told of her fear. "She done went out on the moors late yesterday afternoon, to gather blossoms, one said. She never come back. Her father, he did follow her out, but not a trace of her did he find last night. Was like the devil had swallowed her up."

The devil. The devil. The words rang in Adrienne's ears.

"Go on, Mrs. Fletcher," she said, over the dryness in her throat.

"But they found her body this morning," said the woman, watching Adrienne's face with alert sly eyes. "All ripped to bits she was, the poor little child. Raped and murdered, her throat cut from ear to ear. And slashes all about her little naked body."

Throat cut. Her little naked body. Adrienne forced herself to remain calm outwardly, though she was shaking inside.

"I was very sorry to hear it. Please convey my sorrow to the baker and his wife, and tell them I will send food and flowers to them." And she leaned back in the carriage.

The woman bobbed another curtsey, and backed away again. The coachman drove on slowly. Rosa let out a sigh. A man came up to the coach, looked at Adrienne, whispered, "It was Lord Satan, I'll be bound! It was Lord Satan!"

Her blood seemed to run cold in her body. Rosa started to scold the man roundly. Adrienne hushed her imperiously.

"Do you mean my husband, Lord Vincent Stanton?" she said, quietly. "He is in Bath, on business."

The man backed away, losing his courage. "I just heard—he was seen on the moors—him in his black cloak," he muttered. "You don't know what manner of man you married, my lady!" And he turned and ran down an alley as though demons pursued him.

Behind them came a high-pitched cackle. Adrienne started, and Rosa jumped up and turned about. Granny Dille stood behind the carriage, leaning on her cane, her bright eyes malicious.

"Was Lord Satan, was Lord Satan!" she intoned. "I saw him on the moors! Bloody knife in his hand! Sacrificing to the devils in hell, he was!"

There was a shocked murmur from several women gathered near the stores, they all turned to stare at Granny. Several crossed themselves, muttering.

"The devil—Lord Satan—Lord preserve us. In the name of the father and of the son—Lord help us. Lord help us!"

Adrienne felt faint. "Drive on," she said, curtly. Rosa snapped another order at the coachman, and he whipped up the horses. They turned about, and he started back along the village street toward the road to the castle.

And all along the way, Adrienne was vividly conscious of the stares, the whispers, growing louder, louder, more forceful.

"Lord Satan—they say it was Lord Satan—a devil—he is a devil! Ripped and torn, she was—a bloody sacrifice to the devil! All ripped about and bloody—the devil! Lord Vincent Stanton, it was him as done it—it was him— Lord Vincent done it—they say it was him as done it—"

When they were clear of the village, the coachman swore. "Bloody damn fools!" he said grimly. "Shouldn't have driv' down here. Pack of bloody fools!"

Rosa had her arm about Adrienne, and gently forced her head back on the ample shoulder. "There now, dear lady, don't fret yourself. They doesn't know what they says," she crooned. "Doesn't know anything. Just don't you mind what they says. Oh, my lady, we shouldn't ha' come down here."

"I had—to know. I had—to know," Adrienne whispered.

"Won't get the truth from that pack of fools," said the coachman angrily.

Adrienne lay down again when she had returned. She wished Lady Guinevere would come to her, but the frail little ghost had disappeared for the past several days. Adrienne thought perhaps she had gone to see what her son did in Bath. She had a lively interest in his activities, though she would not visit him or speak to him.

Vincent returned the next day. His arrival was quiet,

and Adrienne did not know he was in the castle until he entered her little study and came up to her smiling.

This time she did not come to greet him. She studied his face with grave inquiring troubled eyes. He was a devil. Could he kill freely, would he kill an innocent girl, a little blonde girl who did no one any harm?

The blood of the innocent, she thought, suddenly. The blood of the innocent. At the altar, the black altar, he had spilled the blood of the innocent, and drank of it. Had he done it again—on the bleak wind-swept moors, taken the life of an innocent young girl, to drink of her blood for his own powers?

She shivered as Vincent touched her, and bent for his kiss. He paused, his face close to hers, the green eyes studying her keenly. Then he drew back.

"What is it? What has happened?" he asked sharply.

She told him flatly, with no words of greeting for him. "Little Flora Moberly was murdered on the moors two nights ago. Raped, murdered, her body ripped to pieces."

"Another one? Hell! There are evil works abroad," he said, scowling, his dark triangular brows meeting over his jade green hard eyes. "She did no one any harm."

"Vincent? I heard talk—you were seen on the moors that night," she said, and bravely met his eyes.

He stared at her blankly. "I was in Bath," he said, inanely, and his mouth twitched. "Lord God, I guess that is no excuse," and did not even seem to realize he had called on God. "You know I can fly anywhere. No, I was not on the moors last night or the night before. Neither was father. He was with me in Bath. We thought mother was there too, we heard her giggle once."

"Vincent," she said, very gravely, very wearily. "I want you to tell me the truth, on my life, on the life of our child. Tell me the truth."

He began to scowl again, heavily. "I have told you the truth," he said, harshly.

"Look into my eyes. Tell me, swear to me on the life of our child, that you did not murder Flora Moberly!"

She put her hands on his arms, looked up into the dark angry flushed face of her husband. He glared down at her, his jade eyes hard as marbles.

"I did not do it! I swear to you on anything you wish! I did not murder Flora Moberly, or any of those girls! Lucifer, what do you think of me? That I murder at whim?"

"I saw you—slit the throat of the girl—on the altar," she said slowly.

"And healed it again on the instant!" he whipped back at her. "That is part of our ceremonies. Not rape of an unwilling girl. I don't need unwilling girls! I can get plenty of willing ones!" And he laughed at her, jeeringly.

She ignored that, though it hurt her. "You deny the murder, then?"

"I deny it! By Lucifer, I deny it!" And he flung himself away from her and stormed from the room, slamming doors behind him, yelling for his valet, raging at the footman for clumsiness.

"By Lucifer—he denies it," she said aloud, sadly to herself. "By—Lucifer—oh, dear God, what shall I do?"

She put her face in her hands, and rubbed her hot forehead. Where was the truth, where was honesty, and most of all, where was the murderer?

She had to do something, she had to know. She could not live with a man who would murder an innocent child. She would die first, and let her unborn child die with her.

She rubbed her arms. She felt cold, chilled to the bone. She picked up a cloak and put it about her, but was still cold.

Dinner that evening was silent. Vincent was scowling at his plate, eating absently, barking a few orders to the footman, otherwise not speaking. She was preoccupied with her thoughts. She slept alone in her bed that night. Vincent had considerately left her alone in the later months of her pregnancy.

By morning, when she wakened, she knew what she was going to do. She waited until Vincent had left his room. She had had her tea and toast in her room.

She dressed warmly, though it was July. She chilled easily, especially in the open carriage, in the wind off the moors.

She went down the stairs, back to the side doors, and out into the stableyard. Only the grooms were there.

In a natural tone, half-smiling, she asked one of them to bring the carriage. They hurried to obey her.

When she was alone in the carriage, with the coachman up top, she told him, "I would go down to the village. There is someone I must talk to."

"But my lady—Rosa—she ought to go—"

111

"I have given her other duties to do this morning," she said, in such a firm tone that he was silenced.

They drove along, and she shivered as she had known she would, in the wind off the moors. She could not keep from glancing again and again off to that bleak desolation. Even on the bright July day, with the sun shining on it, the rocks and crags, the sand and bleak grasses, the few flowers gave it an appearance of being carved out of a piece of hell, and set on earth to make man appreciate his fertile lands and beautiful pastures.

In the village, she ordered the coachman to stop at the silk shop. She got down, with his help, and sent him away to water the horses. Then after he had left, she picked up her skirts, and walked away from the shops, toward the large church, to the house beside it.

She had to consult the priest, she must have his advice. He was, after all, a man of God, trained in the problems of the world. He must help her, she thought. There was no one else in the world who could.

CHAPTER 13

The housekeeper, clad in black, came to the door and let her in. Her impassive face showed no surprise. "I will call Father James Francis," she said, at Adrienne's request for the priest.

The woman showed her into a small study. Adrienne sat down in the bleak small room, thinking how different it was from the luxurious parlor she had seen on her other visit. Only a small crude desk, two chairs, a bookcase crammed full of books, a candleholder were in that room. She glanced curiously at the titles of the books and gave a start of alarm.

She caught titles about demons and devils, witchcraft and black mass, Satanism, along with Bibles, commentaries, books of liturgy and prayer.

What was the priest studying, here? Did he worry about the presence of the devil in his parish? Did he know something about her husband, about Roderick Stanton, about the strange events in the castle, about the black masses held?

The door opened. She turned awkwardly in the straight-backed chair, as the priest came in. She tried to stand. He motioned her kindly to remain.

"No, no, my lady, remain seated. I see you are expecting a blessed event," and he smiled, his eye glowing with kindness. "May I offer you my best wishes for a safe event and a fine child? I shall offer prayers for you."

"Thank you, father," she said meekly. He seemed to be different from her first visit. She had been overwrought, she had probably imagined things.

He seated himself at the small wooden desk and looked across it at her. His fingers, long and slender, played with the rosary and crucifix at his chest. She watched his fingers play with one bead, then the next.

He was clad in black, the black robes of a priest, with the white turned collar. His face was calm under the silvery grey hair. His black eyes were gentle and peaceful today, as though he had found rest for a time from some inner torment.

"Have you been considering my words to you, my lady?" he asked gently, when she remained silent, considering how to approach the problem.

She started, then remembered what he had said. "I have been trying to help the tenants," she said slowly. "I think I am succeeding in bringing my husband to a better understanding of their needs. He has softened toward them, he will listen when I—when we speak of needs and problems."

He nodded, but his face shadowed a little. "Yes, I think he has done a little good," said the priest, as though quite unsatisfied with it.

"I have come on—another matter, Father Francis," she said. "It is about—Flora Moberly. The little girl murdered on the moors."

"Yes, poor child," he said, and sighed deeply. "It will be my sad duty to say her last rites tomorrow morning. Shall you attend the funeral, my lady?"

"I think not," she said quietly. She twisted her fingers on her small reticule, until she realized his alert eyes were watching the signs of unease. She made her fingers

113

lie still on the bag. "There is some talk. That is what concerns me. That, and the murderer."

"Ah, yes, the murderer," he said. "There have been several murders of late on the moors. We must catch the mad killer, must we not? No one is safe until we do."

"Who do you think is doing the killing, father?" she asked. "Do you have any ideas?" She met his black eyes directly with her wide blue eyes.

He hesitated a long fearful moment. "Do you have any ideas, my lady?"

"I have heard gossip in the village, father. They said— it was Lord Satan. They mean my husband, Lord Stanton. But he—I am sure it is not he." She added this with more firmness than conviction.

"You are sure," he said.

"Aren't you sure, father?" She looked at him again. His black eyes were shadowed now by the long dark lashes, as his eyelids drooped. "You have known my husband for several years. I know you have quarreled, but you know him to be—what he is."

She held her breath as the priest seemed to ponder deeply. He finally stirred, and reached out absently for a prayer book on the table. He fingered it, opened it, seemed to read a passage, then closed the small black book again.

"Yes, I do know him—for what he is, my lady. I have tried to tell you gently how he is. I believe he is a devil."

And abruptly the black eyes were looking fully into hers, reading her, she thought. She looked down at her hands, and was proud they were not shaking.

"That is a strange thing to say, father," she said calmly. "He is my husband. He is the son of Roderick Stanton and of Lady Guinevere Stanton, and her family lived in this neighborhood for several hundred years. Castle Caudill and its people are well-known in Cornwall. How can you say he is a devil?"

"I have seen things, I have heard things. They tell of black masses in the crypt of Castle Caudill. They tell of strange beings wandering on the moors. They tell of unusual powers and intelligence in Roderick Stanton and his son Vincent. They are seen in London, then in Bath, and then abroad in Paris or London, or Rome, or Vienna, all in a short time. How can they appear there without flying?"

"My husband has great physical strength and stamina,"

she said. "I have known him to travel from London back to the castle in a day, which would overwhelm an ordinary person with weariness. He changes horses frequently, has them posted along the road, and of course he buys the best horses."

"Of course," said the priest ironically. "He has money as well as power. He buys the best of everything."

She knew she was not mistaken. She had caught the tones of jealousy when he spoke of money and power. He hated her husband, he was intensely jealous of him.

"Yes," continued the priest. "He is able to buy anything he wishes, power, jewelry, even a beautiful wife," and he looked significantly at the silk dress, the long blonde hair, the fur-trimmed velvet cloak, the golden chain and dangling locket of mother-of-pearl and diamonds on her breast.

"I think you insult me, sir," she said, dangerously quiet. "I was a relative of his wife. He brought me to the castle, as he was my guardian. He did me the honor of asking me to marry him, and I consented because I had learned to love him. He is immensely kind to me, and very thoughtful of my every good."

Even as she said the words, she was conscious of the irony behind them. Thoughtful of her good—but he wanted her to participate in black masses, he wanted her to become a devil like himself! And her son, her child, when he came, would be part devil, and Vincent would wish to train him in his devilish and powerful ways.

Her fingers clenched over each other, and the diamond ring on one hand clashed softly with the sapphire ring on the right hand. Vincent's gifts, Vincent's tokens of his ownership of her, his rights over her.

The priest got up abruptly from his chair, and came around the desk. "We spar with words, my lady," he said, abruptly harsh. "I would be done with words which are veiled. I will speak frankly. Your husband is a devil. It is my life's ambition to trap him, to reveal him for what he is! I would expose him and his evil to the world! Ruin him, wreck him, force him to return to the underground hell from whence he came!"

Adrienne shrank back in her chair with a little cry of fear as the priest bent over her. She gazed up at him, her eyes wide and fascinated. "No—no—no," she panted.

"Yes, yes, my lady! He is evil! He is the devil! I have sworn all my life to root out evil, to slash about with my sharp knives of righteousness, and kill with the sword of the Lord! I shall expose him, he shall die, and his evil with him!" The priest was bending over her, close to her, she could smell his strange breath, and fear was sweeping through her and making her faint.

She could smell evil, she could smell heavy sulphur and fire. She was afraid, afraid. She tried to persuade herself that she smelled sulphur because they spoke of the devil, and his presence was here. But it was the priest, the priest—

No, no, it could not be, she thought. She kept fighting her own senses, trying to think, trying to be calm. All she knew was that evil was here, strongly, overwhelmingly.

The priest was whispering to her, hissing the words, his black eyes feverishly bright, his hand reaching out for her hands. She shrank back from him, evading his grasp.

"You will—help me—trap him! You will tell me—all that happens—in the castle! Tell me about the black mass! Tell me how he performs the black mass! Tell me how he does it. Tell me if he drinks the blood of the innocent! Tell me if he uses the communion bread in lewd manner! Tell me what he does on that black altar! Tell me all! Tell me!"

She closed her eyes, half-fainting in the stifling atmosphere of the small study. "No—no—no—"

"Yes, you will help me trap him! You are beautiful, innocent as an angel, yet wise. You will know how to trap him. The innocent trapping the devil himself! How they will praise you! I shall offer prayers for you on the altar of God! You will be a saint, you shall go straight to heaven when you die!" He was hissing, hissing in her ears, and she felt sick.

She pushed away his hands reaching for her. She managed to get out of the chair, but her bulk was making her unsteady. He caught at her elbows, holding her close to his hot black-clad body. She caught again the unmistakable smell of sulphur.

"Yes, you shall help me trap him!" he said firmly, glaring down at her. "You shall help me!"

"I must—go now," she said faintly. She tried to wrench herself from his grasp, she could not, he was holding her so tightly. She felt his heat against her very body, against the bulk that was her child stirring in her belly.

"No, you shall not go!"

116

He seemed to have made up his mind. He drew her with him, out into the hallway, toward the back of the house. She struggled against him, but her strength was like that of a puny child in the grip of a mad giant. He pushed her into a small parlor at the rear of the house.

She sank down on a couch, staring up at him. Had he run mad? His eyes glittered with strange fire, his black eyes shining like coals. "You shall stay here," he said, grinning and nodding his head. "You shall stay here, and you shall decide to help me! I need your help in trapping your husband! And you shall help me!"

He grinned and nodded, and bounced over to the door, slamming it after him. She heard the grind of the lock as he turned the key. She was locked in.

She put her head in her hands. Her head was spinning, her brain was so confused and troubled she did not know what to do.

He was evil, she thought. Or he was mad. Perhaps he was mad. Perhaps the devil had driven him mad. The devil, her husband. Her Vincent.

She sat there for what seemed a long long time. She saw the sunlight streaming into the room, changing directions as the sun moved in the heavens. The room grew warm, and she removed her cloak, and walked about the small decorative parlor, looking curiously at the odd ornaments.

There were strange statuettes about, on the mantel and little tables. Strange carved wood figures, odd porcelain figures, little gods and goddesses with small evil faces drawn in grimaces of hate or pain. On one table she looked at each figure in turn, and found them like nothing she had seen on earth. She dropped one as though it had burned her. It felt like fire in her fingers.

She returned to the couch, put her feet up and tried to rest. Vincent would miss her, the coachman would report her disappearance. He would find her—would he not?

Or did the priest have powers stronger than those of Vincent? Who was stronger, the Lord or the devil? She knew that answer, the Lord was more powerful. But was the priest of the Lord, truly? Was he a man of God, or a man twisted and grown mad with his rage and jealous hate?

She remembered vividly what the woman, the wife of

117

the tenant, had said to her. Can a devil do good? Can a good man do evil?

She did not know.

She was conscious of intense weariness, and put her head down on a pillow to sleep. Vincent would find her, and rescue her. She must rest, and wait, and gather her strength for herself and for her coming child.

She jerked awake as someone bent over her. She opened her eyes, and gasped with a cry of alarm. The grinning witch, Granny Dille, was bending over her.

"There you are, my pretty! Awake now? Yes, you are awake. You will talk to Granny Dille now, won't you? You can't run away from Granny Dille now!" And the old woman cackled, her eyes flashing with insanity. Her grimy hand was reaching out greedily for the gold chain and mother-of-pearl locket. "Pretty, pretty," she said, and fingered it fondly.

Adrienne felt a strong strange impulse to give the chain and locket to the woman. She did not want to, but she felt the impulse. She stifled it firmly. It was Vincent's gift, a love gift to her. Their love was strong between them.

"What do you want, Granny Dille?" she asked quietly.

"Hey, hey, hey!" the woman cackled, and her eyes flashed. "I came to talk to you. Chance to talk to you. You can't run away from me here! Father has you imprisoned here! You can't get away from me now! You have to listen to me here!"

"I will listen to you," said Adrienne, with intense calm, though inwardly she was frightened and far from cool. "What do you wish to say to me?"

"I want some of his powers! I'll help you leave here, if you help me! Fair for fair! Tell me how he flies! Tell me about his black mass! Tell me how to use the herbs he uses! He has powers I want. You shall find out for me, and tell old Granny Dille, so she can grow young again, and powerful! Yes, and rich! Rich! I would fly to the southern countries, and come back with my hands full of emeralds and diamonds!" And she laughed softly her eyes glittering madly.

For a long moment, Adrienne thought of her father-in-law, Roderick Stanton, the true devil, who flew about the world. He had promised her emeralds on the next trip!

The old witch seemed to read her thoughts. "Or have

him bring me emeralds and diamonds," she said eagerly. "I will be satisfied with them—for the time! But there is blood on the moors, blood on the moors, and there must be a blood sacrifice for the blood. Only blood will answer for blood!"

Adrienne shuddered violently, and winced as the old crone reached for her locket again.

"This gold is from strange places," whispered the woman, hissing as the priest had done. "These diamonds, so big and flashing, yes, yes, they are from strange bowels of the earth. From hell itself. Get me some of these diamonds. Give me the locket and chain!"

"No—no—no!" cried Adrienne as the woman yanked violently at her neck in an effort to pull the chain from her.

The priest came into the room. His stern voice sounded from behind the old witch.

"What are you doing, Granny? Get out of here! I told you not to come in with this woman! Get you gone!" And he waved his hand imperiously.

The woman whined, bending over, suddenly stooped and old and powerless. "I did not harm, father, I did no harm! It's only old Granny Dille, wanting a pretty for herself! I want her chain and the diamonds. Get them for me, and I'll give you fresh herbs for healing, fresh powers for healing souls!" And she suddenly cackled wickedly, and was gone.

Adrienne was shuddering with cold and fright. She drew the velvet cloak about her, the fur collar about her throat, hiding the gold locket and gold chain. The blue velvet felt warm to her fingers, and she gathered courage from its warmth. Vincent had given it to her, to keep his lovely warm, he had said.

"She is a wicked woman, father," she said. "She is wicked and evil. You should not let her come here. You should not listen to her!"

The priest stared at her oddly, his full sensuous mouth drawn down in a cynical line. "You think she can influence me?" he asked.

"She is trying to," said Adrienne. "Oh, sir, I beg you, break away from her spells! She is trying to bewitch you! Have nothing to do with her! She is only a minor witch, anyway, and can do little for you of any worth!"

"Who told you she is a minor witch?"

Suddenly, too late, she remembered it was Vincent

119

who had said that Granny Dille was a minor witch, that she had little power to do evil. She flushed, uneasily, and turned her guilty blue eyes away.

"Did my Lord Stanton tell you this?" asked the priest. "Did he tell you? How did he know?"

"I heard gossip," she said, vaguely, picking at the velvet cloak nervously. "I am hungry," she said, to change the subject. "I should like food and water. Better than that, I should like you to call my carriage! I would return to my home!"

"You will not return until you agree to help me on my mission," said the priest curtly. "No food or water until you help me! You shall help me destroy the evil here! I would trap your husband, for he is a devil, and his murders are an outrage! I shall stamp him out, I shall expose him, and the village shall be clean again! The moors shall be clean once more. No more blood, no more blood on the moors!"

She shuddered violently, and lay back wearily on the pillows. "I cannot—help—you" she said, so softly he bent closer to hear her.

"You will feel differently about it—tomorrow—or the next day," he said, with cold significance.

"Not, not tomorrow, not the next day. Never. You do not know me," she said.

"You will not know yourself—after a few days in my care," he said, and he laughed, and left the room. The door was locked behind him.

She was stiff at his final words. After a few days— What would he do to her? What could he do?

She was afraid to think what he meant. She pressed her cold hands to the bulk of her belly, where the child stirred and kicked in her. Would he harm her, would he hurt her coming child? Oh, God, God, God, help me, she thought.

But only evil surrounded her, there was no good that she could find.

CHAPTER 14

Adrienne tried to sleep again, but she could not rest.

She was afraid, coldly afraid, of what might happen to her. And she was hungry and thirsty. She longed for a long cool drink of spring water. Or a hot comforting cup of tea.

She thought about tea at the castle, of one of the maids coming in with a silver tray filled with beautiful blue china. The silver teapot shining and hot and steaming. The cream pot and sugar bowl, all so exquisite and dainty. Herself pouring out tea for Vincent, sitting and chatting with him calmly about matters. Or Vincent telling her enchanting stories of travel and adventure and fantasy.

Vincent, his green eyes gentle, his lips smiling, his devil hiding. Only a husband, with his wife, entertaining her, solicitous for her comfort. She was cared for, warmed and watched over, teased gently, loved, desired, wanted, needed.

Yes, needed, she thought. Vincent needed her to make him more human. He needed her to become better than he had been, to bring out the good that was in him.

"Vincent," she whispered, her eyes closed. "Vincent, Vincent, Vincent, where are you?"

She was concentrating her thoughts on him intensely, wishing for him, needing him, wanting him.

It was scarcely a surprise at first when she heard his voice. It was upraised, yelling, cursing.

Just as when she had heard him first, she thought.

He was cursing in a steady streaming. Then she heard the thud of his boots, coming along the passageway.

"Adrienne!" he yelled, commandingly. "Adrienne, where are you?"

She got up from the couch, slowly because of her coldness and the bulk of herself. "Here," she said, then more loudly, "Here, Vincent! In here!" She went to the door and pounded on it. "I'm locked in here!"

"Stand back from the door," he ordered, his voice harsh.

She stood away. He thudded against it once, twice, then it crashed in, and Vincent stood in the doorway, glaring down at her. She did not care how dreadful his face was in its fury, how flashing his green flaring eyes. She fell against him, clutching him weakly.

"Vincent, you came. Oh, Vincent, you came. Oh, I prayed," she whispered.

His arms closed about her tightly, then more carefully as he felt her shaking. "You called to me. That was what brought me," he said drily, more calmly. "Come, Adrienne. I will take you home now."

"He locked me in," she whispered, looking around him at the scowling face of the priest.

She felt Vincent stiffen against her. He said nothing then, leading her past the priest and his impassive housekeeper, down the hallway to the front door. The coachman waited with the carriage. A small boy held the reins of Vincent's black stallion.

Vincent half-carried her down the stairs. At the carriage, he lifted her up and into the seat, settled her velvet cloak about her, covered her with the rugs. Then he turned to the priest who had followed them out.

A curious crowd had gathered, standing a respectful cautious distance from them. Adrienne saw the grocer and his wife, women from the baker's, several children, Granny Dille leaning on her cane and standing apart from the others, two men from the blacksmith's, several farmers on the edge of the crowd.

Vincent called out as though the priest was some distance from him rather than five feet away. "You—dared to—hold my wife prisoner here! You dared!"

"She came with information. I merely wished to make her comfortable while she spoke," said the priest, smoothly, but his face was paling, and he put his fingers uneasily to his lips.

Vincent raised his right fist to heaven. "I call on Lucifer," he yelled. "I call on Satan himself to curse you and bring you down! I call on Moloch, may he stab your vitals! I call on Belial and his smooth tongue to confound your smooth lying tongue!"

Adrienne gasped in fright, and was not alone. The

crowd of listeners was leaning forward, watching, waiting, their eyes wide and scared and fascinated.

The priest took two steps back, and clutched at his chain and crucifix. "I tell you, I will curse you with the cross of Christ!" he said boldly, glaring at Lord Satan. "This crucifix . . . it will damn you. Damn you—damn you down to the hell from whence you came!"

Vincent flung back his handsome black head, his black eyes glittering, his face darkly saturnine. "Your crucifix is damned! You have fouled it! It has no more power! Its power is gone, with yours!"

The priest held up the crucifix. It caught the silver sunlight and glittered. But Vincent only laughed again, wildly, mockingly.

"It has no power," the man cried. "It has no power! None is left. Cannot you feel the power is gone? Gone! I curse you with all the devils of hell! I call on Mammon whom you have come to worship before all other gods! May he curse you with unfulfilled wishes for money and jewels and power! I call on Beelzebub and his malice! May he rot you in hell, and roast you over the fires!"

The farmers were growling and crossing themselves in fear. The women shrank back. Only Granny Dille stood her ground, chuckling and wheezing, her grey head moving as she looked from one power to the other.

"You cannot curse me with the powers of darkness," said the priest, but he was deadly white, and beads of sweat stood out on his forehead and cheeks. "They have no power over me! My Lord is stronger than they are." He lifted the crucifix again, and moaned a prayer.

Vincent yelled with laughter, his voice echoing through the deadly quiet streets of the village. Adrienne was horribly frightened. She sensed powers lining up to do battle. Vincent had called on the princes of darkness, and she seemed to feel their horrible alien presence there on the village street. It was an eerie horrible tense feeling, and she glanced about uneasily, as though she could see the demons themselves.

"The demons know you well," cried Vincent, and looked about fiercely at the villagers as though he addressed them as well. "The princes of darkness know what evil is going on within this village, and out there on the moors. They will reveal all in their good time! Murders! Blood on the clean beautiful moors! It will be avenged!"

Even the children, small and fascinated, their grimy faces whitening, seemed to sense the evil, and were crossing themselves rapidly. Vincent leaped into the carriage, and gave a curt order. The coachman whipped up the horses. Vincent snapped his fingers at the small boy holding the reins of his horse. The boy jumped forward and put the reins in Vincent's hand, shying violently as his fingers touched Vincent's gloved hand.

The carriage rattled off down over the cobblestones, and the stallion tossed his head impatiently as he was led along with the reins in Vincent's hand. Vincent turned his head, spoke a harsh command, and the stallion quieted.

"Lord Satan," Adrienne caught the whisper. "Lord Satan—he is Lord Satan himself!"

Out of the village, Vincent finally spoke to her. "They will know me before I am through," he threatened grimly, his nostrils flaring like that of his frightened stallion. His eyes were wildly green, flaring red with fury. "They will know I am Lord Satan! They will know me, fear me, and obey me from now on!"

She shuddered in the blue velvet cloak. For once, he did not seem to notice her trembling and fear. He was staring straight ahead, scowling. Once he turned and looked out across the bleak moors, and his look was deadly in its searching, as though he saw horrible things she could not see.

She was weak and shaking, when they reached the castle. He lifted her down, said, "Wait." He turned the stallion over to a groom who came running.

Then he picked up Adrienne, and carried her slowly up the long stone stairs to the castle entrance. He set her down only when he had reached her blue living room. Gently he unfastened her velvet cloak and set it back.

"Have you lunched?" he asked, then, and his tone was almost normal.

"No, Vincent. And I am—so thirsty," her voice broke on the words pathetically. "I longed—for a cold drink. They would not give me food or drink."

"Curse him, curse him!" said Vincent, furiously again. He rang for the maid, ordered tea and meat and sweets to be brought at once. He brought her water with his own hands, and held her up while she drank.

Then he laid her gently down on the couch again, and smoothed her mussed blonde hair.

"Little one, never leave me again. I have gone mad,

I think," he said quietly, with a ring of hard command behind the smooth tone. "Never—never—leave me again. I shall commit murder on anyone who dares take you from me!"

"That is the spirit, my son," said a familiar drawling tone. And Lord Roderick Stanton appeared, sitting in a nearby chair, his black cloak flung back from his black-clad body. His riding boots were dusty, his face was weary. "I came from quite a distance to see you, Adrienne. What mischief are you up to? Would you betray us?"

"No, sir, I think not, sir," she said, meekly. "I was only—trying to find out—who killed Flora Moberly."

Roderick Stanton waved his languid hand. "A chit. She does not matter. The priest is possessed, Vincent. You must get rid of him. I told you that before. Destroy him with fire. You can. I showed you the trick of it many times."

The maid brought tea, showed surprise on seeing Lord Roderick, curtsied, and said she would bring more tea.

Adrienne sat up slowly to serve them. The familiar ceremony was helping restore her to calm. But her father-in-law worried her. He was so grim, so hard, his black eyes flashing.

"I told you before, destroy the priest with fire. He is far gone in evil works. He conspires with the witch, Granny Dille. Destroy him," said Roderick, sipping his tea calmly.

Adrienne watched him with fascinated eyes. Vincent shook his head, frowned.

"He is supposed to be a man of God. I am not sure in my mind if God has touched him with madness, or if the evil has truly entered his soul. Do we have reports on him from Satan?" asked Vincent, as calmly as though he asked for a report on a farm from a tenant.

"Who needs reports? And these things take time. There must be an investigation. The priest is cunning, and every day he serves mass, invoking the gods he worships. It is hard to get past his surface."

"Then we must wait."

Roderick grew impatient. Adrienne was munching hungrily on a sandwich of cold meat and cheese, drinking the good hot tea, dipping into a pastry of chocolate and whipped cream at the same time. She was so hungry and so thirsty, she thought she would never be satisfied.

Roderick waved his smooth white hands, then reached

125

for the teacup again. "Delicious tea, my dear daughter," he said mildly, to Adrienne. "You make as good tea as my Guinevere. She was the best tea-maker I knew. Just the right amount of cream and sugar, just the right strength."

"Thank you, dear father," she said, and smiled shyly at him.

He smiled down at her, with unexpected kindness, and patted her hand near him. The touch warmed her, but did not burn.

"I have brought you more pretties, as I said I would," he told her. He dipped into one pocket, and poured out a handful into her lap. Green glittered, and blue, and white fire. She gasped, as she stirred and dipped into the mass of gems. Emeralds, and sapphires and diamonds of the finest hue.

He dipped into another pocket, grunted, "I had it here somewhere, picked it up in France. Here you are, dear." And he put a small box into her lap. "Snuff box—not that you will use it. Put some earrings into it."

It was a circular snuff box, carved in gold, with a miniature on the top of it, of a fine lady with a lute in her hands. She turned it over and over, admiringly. "How very pretty, dear father. I shall cherish it because you brought it to me. But indeed, you must not keep bringing me presents. I dearly love for you to come, just yourself," she said, a little reprovingly.

He smiled, that cynical quirk that drew down the corner of his sensuous mouth, so like Vincent's. "Presents will ensure that I am always welcome, I hope, my dear Adrienne! But they cost me nothing. I just make more money and pick up more gold somewhere to pay for the trifles! Oh, Brazil has hit on another find in emeralds, dear Vincent. You must fly down there and pick up some of the large ones while they are to be had."

"Perhaps later," said Vincent absently, still frowning down at his cup. "Not till after Adrienne has the child, and is quite recovered and well again. I do not want to leave her right now. But father, what about the priest?"

"Burn him with fire," said Roderick, drinking the last tea in his cup. "We can set fire to his house. He will burn up in it, and all his familiars."

Adrienne cried out, and spilled the gems in her lap. They fell to the floor and the sofa in a glittering array of sparkling jewels. "No—no—no! How horrible! You cannot do that, Vincent! You cannot hurt innocent people!"

"Those people are not innocent," said Roderick. "You could clean out the whole village, Vincent. I have been observing them. Lying, cheating, stealing. Saw one mother beating her child. I fixed her for a time, she has a crippling in her limbs now." And he nodded with satisfaction. He explained to Adrienne, "I learned to love children from Guinevere and my experience with Vincent, little devil though he was, and hard to control. If there is one thing which makes the demon rise in me, it is cruelty to small innocent children! And the murders on the moors—" He shook his handsome head, and his face set bleakly.

"But you cannot destroy them with fire!" pleaded Adrienne. "Not all the families—the fathers and mothers and small children—" And she looked at him hopefully.

"Better to clean them all out, and start again. Vincent, I know some witches and warlocks, a whole community longing to move from Ireland. Things have become difficult for them there. They will come in and take the forms of the villagers after you burn everyone with fire. Start over again with people we can be sure of, as we did in the castle when you were a baby. That way there will be no trouble."

"No—no," said Adrienne weakly, and finally lay back on the sofa, her appetite gone. She could have wept. What strength did she have against these two powerful devils? They thought nothing of destroying a whole village full of people, and all the tenants on the farms, everyone around, because they were angry.

In her lonely bed that night, she called softly to Lady Guinevere. "I need you, please come and talk to me, my dear mother!"

To her relief, the little ghost came at once, and settled herself on the bedside comfortably. Her hand soothed Adrienne's fevered face with its little cool fingers.

"There, dear, there, dear, what a dreadful time you had, to be sure! Relax, you are alright now. Vincent will not let anyone harm you."

"He is so good to me," sighed Adrienne. "But did you hear him and his father talking? They speak of destroying the whole village."

"Yes, with the Satanic friends and powers," nodded Guinevere. Her little shining face was sad. "They did that when Vincent was little. Some of the servants were

127

frightened and upset when they began to realize Roderick had demonic powers. They began to talk it about, and people began to call him Lord Satan. So Roderick called on Satan and Moloch and some others, and wiped them all clean. I cried for weeks, and Roderick could not comfort me. Not that he tried hard, he was a brazen bully in those days! Only later was he tender toward me."

"But what can I do? Shall I try to stop them?" asked Adrienne. "Vincent seems bent on destroying."

"Yes, you must," said his mother firmly. "You must stop him. If he does this, the evil in him will increase to a dreadful stage. Oh, dear, I had forgotten that!" And she became quite agitated. "I have been so long away from the world and its opinions. Once evil, real evil, has been done, it increases, and the talk increases. All the world knew eventually that the servants here were gone, and new ones in their place. And talk was whispered about, gossip made, and few people were willing to risk coming here! And the people of the village—they do not deserve to be sent to hell!"

"Sent to—hell!" gasped Adrienne.

"Yes. When they destroy all with fire, all go right to hell, into the power of Satan. Oh, Adrienne, you must stop them. You can influence Vincent. And Roderick seems to have become fond of you, he might listen to you. But your best recourse is to beg Vincent not to bring down fire. It will be scandalous," she added, rather primly.

"Oh, dear," said Adrienne plaintively. She leaned back into the thick pillows with a deep sigh. "I don't know what to do, truly, mother!"

"You must stop Vincent! It is bad for the village, worse for my dearest boy Vincent. I don't want the evil in him to increase. And you are such a good influence on him, Adrienne! Do try hard! Don't let him do evil!"

"I will try to stop him," she promised simply. The ghost faded away slowly, patting her hand right up to the moment of disappearing.

Vincent came in, his robe fastened about him. "Can't you sleep, love?"

"No, I wish you would hold me, and keep the nightmares away," she asked, and turned to him as he came into her bed. He held her so gently, so securely, that she drew a deep sigh of relief, and relaxed, and went to sleep.

CHAPTER 15

Roderick Stanton was still there the next day. When Adrienne went down to the dining room for breakfast she heard their voices.

She went into the room. Both men sprang up. She thought, "How handsome they both are," and smiled at them shyly, with pleasure.

Vincent came around to hold her chair, and brush his cheek against hers as she seated herself. "How are you, my love?" he asked fondly.

"Pretty well today, thank you. Father, I hope someone prepared a room for you. I am afraid I neglected to give orders," she added with some concern.

"Don't trouble yourself, my dear. Mrs. Griffith always has a room ready for me. And I slept well. I traveled all the way from Brazil, you know," he added, in his calm drawl, reaching for a fresh hot biscuit. "Got the news of trouble, and flew back."

Adrienne stirred her hot tea thoughtfully. A year ago, such conversation would have upset her dreadfully. Now, she just nodded and listened.

The conversation turned again to burning. Vincent seemed more interested, she thought, and was troubled. After breakfast, she asked him to take her for a walk in the garden.

He brought her cloak, though the day was warmer than usual, and the sunshine shone golden through the trees and across the rippling blue lake. They strolled along the paths of flowers, the red and white roses, the yellow daisies and pink columbine, and the garden pinks she loved. Vincent bent to choose carefully from the pinks, and triumphantly presented her with a choice fragrant bloom.

She put it to her nose thoughtfully. The scent gave her courage.

"Vincent, it distresses me very much when you and your father speak of burning all the people," she said, as

129

calmly as possible. "I talked with your mother about it. She does not wish it either. She said it causes too much talk."

He frowned, his eyebrows drawing down heavily. His arm tensed in her arm. "Do not trouble yourself about it, Adrienne," he said, crisply. "Father and I will decide about it."

"I wish you would not do anything," she said again, gently. "I do not want things to be disturbed about here. Eventually, it will be discovered who the murderer is, and he will be punished. But do not precipitate more trouble in the effort to solve it. That is not—" she hesitated. She wanted to say "right." She finished, "That is not wise."

"The priest tried to harm you. I will kill him for this," he said, and his scowl was bitter and his green eyes hard as jade. "He will not harm me or mine!"

"You came to me, Vincent," she said, and put her face against his upper arm. "I called to you silently, and you came. As long as you always come to me, and save me, and protect me, who can harm me? I am not afraid now."

He put his arms about her, and held her gently against him. She rested her face against his shoulder contentedly, and he could feel, she thought, how happy she was with him. His hand brushed against her thick blonde hair.

"Well, we will consider the matter," he finally said, his voice more controlled. "But you must not interfere in matters of this nature, Adrienne. They do not ultimately concern you."

She drew back a little, and gazed up into his face. "Yes, Vincent, they do concern me. I am your wife, I am Lady Stanton, of Castle Caudill. What happens here affects me. If you make these dread changes, wiping out people with fire, bringing in strangers from Ireland, it will be known! It will be found out! And we will all suffer for it, you and I, and our child."

His face altered sharply when she said the word "child." He gazed down at her thoughtfully, then out over the rippling blue lake. She thought his eyes were more soft and gentle.

Suddenly Roderick Stanton appeared beside them. He was wearing his black velvet cloak, his black suit. Today he wore brilliant emeralds at his throat and wrists, emeralds set in a strange shining silver.

"Is she softening you, Vincent, my boy?" he asked, and

laughed, his eyes sparkling, the lines beside them crinkling up. "I warned you she would try! She is very like your mother! They will soften you up, make you weak!"

"I do not want him weak, my lord," said Adrienne, with spirit. "I do not want him to harm people! I think he does not usually harm people. He is kind. I would not have him destroy people, and ultimately hurt *us*, me and the child."

"The child, the child," said Roderick, rather impatiently, but his hand as he touched her hand was curiously tender. "How you women weave your spells! Even the devil is not immune against a woman and her child!"

"Yes, she weaves powerful spells," said Vincent, and his smile flashed down at her. "The first moment I saw her, she caught me in a strong net."

"And you did not even struggle," said Roderick, and laughed aloud, a ringing laugh that echoed joyously over the lake. "Ah, well, if that is your decision, I am not needed here. I am returning to Brazil today, children. If you need me, send for me, in the usual way, Vincent. I shall come! But I warn you, I shan't be soft again!"

And he disappeared abruptly before they could even wish him farewell. Adrienne called after him, into the empty space, "Safe journey, father!"

Vincent looked at her, his eyes twinkling. "He is always safe, love. What did you think?"

"It does not hurt to send good wishes," she said, with dignity, then hugged his arm to her. "Ah, let us walk. The day is so lovely, Vincent! Have you ever seen the trees so beautiful, the flowers so sweetly pretty, the swans on the lake so soft and black and shining?"

"Beauty is in the eyes of my love," he said, and they walked quite contentedly about the lake and grounds until she was weary.

All was peaceful for the next several weeks. Adrienne found it more and more of an effort to walk about, though Guinevere visited her more frequently and urged her to walk in the gardens.

She was lying on the sofa, half-asleep, in the late afternoon, during the last week of August. She expected the child in two more weeks, and was growing anxious to have it. The bulk was almost too much for her slim body to carry.

She heard Rosa talking to the footman, and turned uneasily on the couch. She had a vague memory of the last

131

time she had heard them talking, and it had caused trouble. She was more than uneasy as they continued.

"Murder—blood on the moors—" Rosa said. "Oh, will it ever end? More and more often they come!"

"Not dead this time—not dead—still alive, heard her screaming—the girl—" The footman's tone dropped, and they muttered and whispered.

Adrienne sat up sharply, and turned dizzy. She put her hand to her head. "Rosa," she said, and called again. "Rosa! Come here!"

"It's the mistress, did she hear us? Oh, dear!" Rosa sounded agitated. The two of them peered into the room.

"Come in here!" said Adrienne, sharply, in her distress. "Both of you! Come in!"

The footman and Rosa came into the room, slowly, their faces almost identical in their apprehension.

"Tell me what has happened. Is it another murder? Who was hurt?"

Rosa finally spoke, because the footman had turned dumb. He was a young man, green, awkward, and Vincent was often impatient with him.

"Well, it is this way, my lady," said Rosa. She twisted her hands in her apron anxiously, studying Adrienne's face for signs of distress. "It's Jennie Tyson."

"Tyson. The second farm near the moors."

"Yes, my lady. Little Jennie, she is about thirteen now, and very pretty. Dark hair and blue eyes. She was raped and someone tried to strangle her, she said. She is cut about and ripped up, but she ain't dead yet."

Adrienne stared up at Rosa. "What happened? How did she escape?"

"No one seems to know, my lady. A farmer found her on the road near the moors. She was screaming and crying out, and he saw a black figure in a black cloak beyond her, waving at him. And the farmer got down from his wagon, and picked up Jennie and druv her in to town to the midwife. She took care of her and sent out the word."

"When did this happen?"

"Last night, about dusk, ma'am."

"Where is Jennie Tyson now?"

"Well, her folks come for her, and took her home. They do be praying over her, but they won't send for the priest, as they and the priest did have words last year."

Adrienne lay back. She had to think. "Very well, Rosa,

thank you for telling me," she said quietly. "I will be alone now." And she closed her eyes as though she would sleep.

Rosa and the footman withdrew from the room, and she heard them muttering fearfully in the hallway.

She was thinking, thinking. If Jennie had seen her attacker, and could identify him, this would solve the murders. She must talk to Jennie, persuade her to talk. Get the words from her. Who was the man in the black cloak? Who had attacked her? She had to know. She had to be sure, she knew it, she had to be very sure it was not Vincent.

She finally got up, and put the blue velvet cloak about her. Today she was wearing a dark blue wool dress, for the rain had come and turned the house chill. She must go—go—somehow she must find the strength to go.

She went out one of the side doors, where there were fewer steps. It was turning dusk. Tea would be served soon—but she could not wait. She must go. In her mind was room for only one thought: she must talk to Jennie Tyson and get the truth from her.

Only the truth would clear Vincent—in the eyes of the world, and in her own mind.

She had to go, she had to go.

She felt as though she were driven by an agony. Another murder on the moors—Jennie might not live—another girl rent and torn by some strange monster of a person. The truth must be found. The truth must out!

In the stableyard, one of the grooms came out in the rain, and paused to gawk at her. "My lady," he finally said.

"Get me a sturdy older horse, one that is steady," she said, firmly. "I will ride."

He was a rather simple man, a little odd in the head, Vincent had said, though good with horses. He frowned, scratched his grizzled cheeks, said, "All right, my lady," and went to get a horse.

He returned with an older mare, saddled and bridled. He helped Adrienne up, no mean task. "You wants me to ride with you, my lady?" he asked.

"No. I will manage," she said, firmly. She was not at all sure, now that she was up on the mare, that she could make it at all. But she must, must, must manage somehow.

The rain came on more heavily, soon soaking through her cloak and into the wool dress. She rode heavily, but the mare carried her at a gentle pace. She kept thinking, "the second farm beyond the moors—second farm, Tyson —Jennie Tyson—"

And the need drove her on, and on.

The mare found the path out to the moors, and she went along, almost subconsciously guiding the mare in the right direction. On the edge of the moors, she glanced out and shuddered heavily. A storm was approaching from the west, and she could see the thick scudding clouds as they rolled across the skies. Far in the distance the lightning flashed, and thunder began to growl.

"Go on, go on," she urged the mare, and the mare broke into a trot. "Oh, no, no," she said, and tried to pull it down. But the mare had turned skittish, veering at shadows, tossing its head impatiently. It wanted to turn back to the safety of the warm stables.

Adrienne would not let it turn about. She urged it firmly onward. The mare was trotting faster now, and Adrienne was jolted about. She felt the child turn over inside her, and felt a thrill of fear.

It was farther than she had thought. In the carriage, with Vincent driving, it had not seemed far at all. She was tiring fast, and frightened. But she had to see Jennie Tyson, she had to talk to her.

Only Jennie Tyson had a clue as to who the murderer was. Only she could solve the murders on the moors, the problem of who spilled the blood on the moors.

"Go on," she whispered to the mare, leaning heavily forward on the pommel. "Go on—go on—please—go on—"

The clouds drew overhead, thick and black, and heavy with rain. The rain poured down in a burst of fury. Lightning flashed, the white jagged streaks piercing the black sky.

Then a particularly close streak, the mare screamed and reared straight up. Adrienne felt herself falling, caught at the saddle, could not catch it, and fell. Fell from the saddle, her foot caught, then wrenched loose.

She lay where she had fallen. The mare was trotting off down the road, heading for the stables. Adrienne groaned. She was jolted cold. She stirred feebly, put her hand to her head, her fingers were bloody.

"Oh—no—I must see—Jennie Tyson," she muttered, and fell back in a faint.

Much later she wakened, cold, wet, aching all over

134

her body. Vincent was carrying her. She was surprised about that. Why was she so cold and wet? Had she fallen in the lake? The sky was black, the rains pouring down, and Vincent was cursing.

"Vincent, I must see—Jennie Tyson—" she said. "Vincent, I must—see—Jennie—Tyson—"

Vincent said curtly to someone, "She is raving, she is feverish. I can't understand what she says."

"Oh, Lord, sir, I think the baby is coming," cried Rosa, and cradled Adrienne on her lap as Vincent lifted her into the carriage.

"We'll get her home. Help her, Rosa!" And Adrienne felt the great wrench in her body, as the pains came again.

She blacked out again, recovered, saw Vincent's face as he bent over her, his eyes very green and troubled. She tried to reassure him, but the pains wrenched her, and she cried out. The blackness closed in again and again, like waves of dark storms flaring through her body and her mind.

Later someone lifted her, and put a gold cup to her lips. "Drink, darling, it will help," said Vincent's voice. She tried to push the cup away. It was something about the black mass, she would not take part in the black mass, she thought. "It is wine, darling, it will relax you."

He persisted gently, and she had to give in and drink. His will was so much stronger than hers, she decided, feebly. She drank the warm wine, and lay back, sighing.

"There, now the babe is coming at last," whispered Rosa. "There—now—it comes——"

And her body was wrenched, and pain filled her, and she sobbed, and all was black again.

It was a long time before she wakened. She opened her eyes to sunshine, and seeing Rosa nodding in a chair beside the bed. She felt weak and spent, her body ached. She put her hand automatically, anxiously to her stomach.

The baby was gone! She had lost the child! "Oh, no—no—" she whispered. Some memories came back, the rain, the mare, blackness on the moors, the lightning streaking across the sky. She began to sob. "I lost—the baby—oh—oh—"

Rosa waked with a jerk, and stared at her in alarm. "Oh, my lady, you're awake at last. Now, don't cry, my lady, don't cry—oh, dear, I had best get the master—"

And she ran out of the room, and returned with Vincent. Vincent looked odd, thought Adrienne, staring at him through her tears. He looked exhausted, human, cross, unshaven, with only a robe over his nightrobe, in the middle of the sunny day.

"I have to—see—Jennie Tyson," sobbed Adrienne.

Vincent stared down at her. And he shook his head. "Of all the obstinate, headstrong, wilfull, devious, tricky, witch of a woman—you are all!"

"I have to—see her—" she said. "And I have—lost—my baby—oh, Vincent," and she began to sob bitterly, turning her face feebly toward the pillow.

He sat down cautiously beside her, and stroked his hand gently down over her arm. "No, you didn't, love. We have him safe and warm. Shall I bring our little wee one to you?"

Her sobs stopped. She gazed at him through blue drenched eyes.

"Safe?" she whispered.

He smiled down at her, a big grin. "Safe. And such a big boy he is, just like his father. But he has your blue eyes."

And he got up, and went into the other room. He returned with a small thing wrapped in a blue blanket, and he gently put the bundle down into her arm. She lifted herself feebly, and he helped her, so she could look down into the small sleeping face.

"Oh—a boy. Oh, Vincent. He came. A miracle!" And she stared and stared at the handsome tiny babe. One little fist waved vaguely in the air. Vincent touched it with his big forefinger, and it showed how tiny the one was.

"A boy," he said, with intense satisfaction. "A sturdy fine elegant boy. You always do things right, Adrienne—even though your heart does lead you astray into wild things, like a ride on horseback through a storm!"

"I had to see—Jennie Tyson—"

His face seemed to close up. He looked away from the child. "Jennie Tyson died in the night," he said, quietly. "She died without revealing the name or identity of her attacker."

Adrienne lay back with a sigh of great disappointment. "Oh, I had—hoped—this time—oh, Vincent, who can it be?"

He did not answer. He lifted the small babe, and took him back to the other room. When he returned, he carried a gold cup, a familiar gold cup. He sat down beside her, lifted her, and said, firmly, "And now you are going to drink this, and sleep all night, my dearest! You must get your strength back."

She drank, and lay back. But she could not sleep well. Fevers came, and drained her of her frail remaining strength. She tossed and turned, and moaned, and spoke of the blood on the moors. The little ghost of Guinevere Stanton came often and bent anxiously over her, but Adrienne did not know her for a long time. Days and nights passed.

Finally one day, Vincent was sitting beside her patiently, talking to her, and she finally opened her eyes and knew him.

He understood at once, and smiled. "You are yourself again, darling," he said, and stroked back the limp blonde hair from her weary thin face.

"Yes, you are—Vincent," she said, and touched his cheek with one finger. "Did I dream—or did the—babe—come? He is a boy?"

To her surprise, there were tears in his green eyes. The first time she had seen tears there. He bent over and brushed his cheek very gently against hers. "Yes, we have a son, love. A fine boy, who is anxious to get to know his mother."

No one could have been more tender to her in the next days, she thought. Rosa told her of his devotion to her night and day during the feverish illness which had possessed her following the birth. Now, he carried her downstairs, stayed with her, talked to her, amused her, brought her the baby, discussed the name endlessly, deferred to her.

He seemed to have lost all his arrogance and fire, she thought, until she heard him one day heartily cursing his valet. She had to smile, she had thought he had lost his vocabulary! But he had it, with improvement and embellishments.

When Vincent returned to her, she said, "I think I have decided on the name for him, Vincent. With your permission, of course."

"Yes, love, what is it?" He sat down beside her, and took her thin hand in his, and caressed it with his lips.

"Vincent—for you. Jonathan—for my father. And Roderick—for your father. Vincent Jonathan Roderick, and Stanton. That is a grand name for such a wee one, but he will grow up tall and strong one day," she sighed with satisfaction.

"Do not forget Lord of Devereux, Lord of Caudill, Viscount Desmond, and all the rest of his titles," Vincent reminded her with a twinkle.

She squeezed his hand as hard as she could. He would be named all those names—but not baptized. He could not be baptized. He was the son of a devil, the devil she loved and adored—even though she did not know whether or not he was capable of murder.

CHAPTER 16

It was a golden day in September. Adrienne had just been contemplating her son with great satisfaction and surprise because he had seemed to smile at her, and him only three weeks old. She set him back in the small basket beside her on the couch, and looked around the room.

Sunlight streamed in the long French windows. Beyond she could see the glory of the early autumn day. A few leaves had turned on the oak trees. The rain had cleared. Maybe she could take little Vincent Jonathan outdoors today, she thought. They had taken him outside for his first outing two days before, then yesterday had been so rainy they had not.

But today was glorious. She would ask Vincent—

Her thoughts were interrupted by loud voices in the hallway. Vincent, cursing. Other voices, as deep and commanding, and noisy and cursing also. She grimaced. What now?

She got up and went to the doorway, to fall back in dismay. The priest was there, black and angry, his face suffused with blood, his grey hair wildly windblown. Beside him was a stranger in a uniform.

Vincent heard her and turned. His green eyes were blazing with fury such as she had not seen in weeks.

The priest spoke to her. "My lady, I have evidence at last! You would be wise to speak now!"

"Speak—about what?" She asked the question, but

knew the answer by the chilling sensation around her heart.

The stranger answered for the priest. "I have arrested my lord Vincent Stanton, Lord of Caudill, Lord Devereux," he said in heavy uneasy accents, his gaze shifting from her eyes, "for the murders on the moors. Especially the murder of one Jennie Tyson."

"No," said Adrienne. "And no again! He did not do it! He is not a murderer!"

"I brought the sheriff here to arrest my lord," said the priest triumphantly. His black eyes glittered strangely. "Jennie told me before she died that it was the devil, Lord Satan, known here as Lord Stanton! She told me with her own lips!"

Adrienne thought, instantly, he is lying! Rosa had told her the family would not send for the priest, they had quarreled with the priest. Yet—yet he might have been sent for, in their desperation— No. He is lying, she thought. She knew he was lying.

"You see," the priest was continuing, "I have known for some time that Lord Devereux was a devil. No one would listen to me. But I knew it, I knew it! And now it is confirmed. He will go on trial for his life, and he shall die for his crimes!"

"Never," said Vincent, in a coldly dangerous tone. "Never, never! It shall never happen!"

"You shall go to prison, you shall be tried! And you will be found guilty, and die!" proclaimed the priest.

The sheriff shifted uneasily, his heavy bulk going from one leg to the other, his hands searching in vain for somewhere to rest, so that he seemed to flutter. "Well, now, that is for the law to decide, begging your pardon, father. He goes to trial, is accused, and witnesses brought in evidence. Then the jury decides about his fate."

"He will be found guilty! My evidence along with others will hang him!"

Adrienne was shuddering in fear. He seemed so very sure. She glanced at her husband, and started in fresh new fear. His green eyes were glittering red as coals, with fire in their depths like fire-opals. He was in a fury of rage. He would bring down fire on them, he would kill them! Then there would be the devil to pay, she thought, and wanted to laugh hysterically.

"We will have to take you off to the jail, my lord," said the sheriff, and reached out his hand to Vincent's arm.

Vincent jerked back, his eyes glittering.

"No," said Adrienne quickly. "He does not need to go to jail." It would be the last blow to that proud man, she thought, wildly. He would never submit to be put in jail, to have watchers come to see him curiously, to be stared at and gossiped about. No, he would never submit to being under restraints. "There is no need," she added quietly. "He will give his word that he will appear at the trial. The word of a Stanton is good."

She looked at her husband appealingly. He was frowning heavily.

"He will not give his word, or keep it if he gives it!" the priest pronounced loudly. His white hands were shaking. "Arrest him, we will carry him off! I warn you, my lord, we have strong men outside who will take you away, conscious or unconscious. You shall be unmasked for the devil you are!"

Adrienne put her hand on Vincent's arm, and felt the tension there. He was leaping to spring. "No, darling, no, remember our child," she said quietly. "All will be well. I promise for him, sir, that my husband will be at his trial. And he shall be vindicated, and the murderer unmasked in time."

"You promise too much," said the priest, his tone becoming shrill and hysterical. His body jerked, beyond control, and she watched fascinated, the little tic at the corner of his sensuous mouth as it jerked, jerked again. "You cannot promise he will come. He is a devil, he will fly away and you will never see him again."

"He will come," she said, holding Vincent's arm in her fingers.

The sheriff shifted his feet again, looking from one to the other. "I accept the lady's word," he said, at last, with evident relief. He had not relished the task of dragging a powerful and wealthy man off to prison, devil or no devil. "You promise he will come to his trial, my lady. That is good enough for me."

"The trial will be at once!" said the priest. "While all is fresh in people's minds. It will be at once!"

"Tell us the day, we will be there." said Adrienne.

The priest looked at the sheriff. "This is Friday. It shall be next Monday, and on Sunday I shall pray heavily for the man's soul!"

Vincent jerked in her hands. "You—pray! Pray to the

devils in hell," he snarled. "They will have you soon enough!"

"Vincent!" Adrienne hushed him gently. "We will come," she said to the sheriff. "On Monday, we shall be there."

The sheriff turned to leave. The priest reluctantly followed, turned about as though to add something, shook his head wildly, and ran down the wide stairs to the waiting carriage.

The sheriff was wiping his forehead, though the day was cool. Vincent watched them go, his eyes jade green.

"I'll send for father," he said, with ominous cold tone. "We'll wipe them all out! Burn them with fire!"

"No, Vincent, no! You shall go to the trial, but you will not be found guilty. You did not murder those girls! You will be found innocent!" She looked up at him pleadingly, wanting him to reassure her.

He did not. His rage was invading his very soul, turning the devil in him to hot rage. "Fire—fire—fire," he muttered. "I'll send for father—between us we can wipe them all out. They will be sorry for putting the blame for this on me! I have never killed a soul—I do other powerful acts, not murder! I do not murder!"

She believed him, and sank against him in utmost relief. She held as much of him as she could get into her small arms. "Oh, Vincent, I love you so much. Believe, believe in me, believe in our child, believe in yourself! We shall win the case, and others will believe in you also! There is much good in you, my darling! They shall know it also!"

His arms held her, but he was not with her, she knew it. "Good?" he muttered. "They will know what powers a devil has. I shall send for father—"

"No, no, do not disturb him. You know how anxious he is to get all those emeralds and the diamonds before they are snatched up," she said, urgently. "And—and think how pleased he will be if you can handle it all yourself!"

"I'll call on Satan himself, and Belial, and Moloch—"

She put her fingers over his lips, and almost snatched them away again. The touch of his mouth was burning her fingers. She held them there with an effort, until his lips had cooled, and his body relaxed somewhat. He kissed her fingers remorsefully.

"I am sorry, darling. I am very enraged," he said, more calmly. "The gall of that priest infuriates me."

"That is what he wants," she said. "He wants to enrage

you, to make you show your devilish powers. Then he will trap you. That is what he really wants. He cannot believe you committed the murders on the moors."

"I wish we would get a report from Satan on the priest," said Viencent, frowning. "I will urge more speed on this matter. They have to get past his masks."

They returned to the living room. Vincent would speak calmly on the matter, then rage would flood through him, and he would curse the priest and the villagers and the sheriff and all who oppose him. She was more and more frantic.

She must save Vincent and his soul, before he did something terrible in his rage.

He was so angry, he was unreasonable. He would bring down hellfire—and trap himself. Because they would know then that he was truly a devil. The secret would be known.

Now the villagers and tenants and officials of the town only guessed that Vincent and his father possessed supernatural powers. They only knew that the two lords had unusual knowledge, of the land and of people. They only knew that Vincent could travel very swiftly. They thought Roderick was dead. If Roderick returned, and helped Vincent bring forth fire—

She shuddered. It would become known, she was sure of it. Something like this could not be hidden forever. It would be known, and they would be hounded from then on, she and Vincent and little Vincent Jonathan, now peacefully sleeping in his small white bed.

What could she do?

Who would know? What evidence was there? Had anyone ever seen someone on the moors?

She went over and over the facts she knew. They were so meager. The girls who had died. The farmer who had picked up small pitiful Jennie Tyson, and had seen a black figure waving at him.

The farmer. She stared into the fire and thought. If the farmer had seen the figure clearly—would he give evidence? But was the figure one of the murderer? Or someone who had tried to help Jennie?

How could she find out the truth? What was the truth?

All those girls murdered, young girls, raped, slit with knives, tortured on the moors. Blood on the moors.

She thought of Granny Dille, cackling as she leaned on her cane. She had known the murderer would strike again.

How had she known? Did she possess powers that Vincent did not have? But Vincent had said Granny Dille was a minor witch, incapable of much power. So how did Granny Dille know that more murders would take place—

Unless Granny Dille had encouraged the murders. Or helped in the murders. Or participated in them, as part of an attempt at black mass on the moors.

Had it been Vincent with her? No, no, her soul cried out. Not Vincent. No, he would not do that. He had said he would not commit murder. He would not. He was even softer and more gentle and tender since the birth of their child. Sometimes when he bent over the crib and studied the tiny crumpled face of his son, his face was lit with a glorious light which was not of the devil, she thought.

He was more gentle, more human now. He had good in him, and it was showing now. She must hope, she must have faith in him. She must help him somehow.

She must help him, find help for him, find someone to give evidence for him. She must find someone who had witnessed one or more of the murders.

Perhaps there were people who had seen something on the moors and were too terrified to tell. She must find them, get them to tell—before it was too late for all of them.

She had to find help—before Vincent did something terrible in his rage, and destroyed them all.

CHAPTER 17

Adrienne started out early the next morning, when she was sure that Vincent was safely working in his study. He still muttered with rage when he spoke of the trial, but he was putting affairs in order to be free on Monday.

He would not go to prison, they both knew it, but did

not speak of it. If he was tried and found guilty, he would disappear and bring fire down on them in his rage.

Then all would be lost of Adrienne's peaceful life. Nothing would ever be the same again, she knew it. She must go with him, to the life of a wandering devil, and take their son with them. She did not know how long she could live. She would die of it, she knew.

Vincent had not thought that far, he was strong, he did not consider her own weakness. He was not inconsiderate. It was just that he was so strong, he did not realize a woman could be weak and frail. But Adrienne knew how she was, and how little she could endure.

She must save Vincent, and herself, and her son.

She ordered a groom to bring out a carriage, and to drive her. She set out for the first farm of a tenant. When she got there, the woman came out to greet her, her face troubled. It was one of the wiser more intelligent women.

"I came to ask your help," said Adrienne, at once, as the groom helped her down. "Come over here and speak with me."

The woman came at once, to lean with her against a fence and look out over the pastures. "I have heard, my lady, that my lord is accused of the moors murders."

"He did not do it," said Adrienne, with quiet conviction. "I am asking your help, and the help of all those who know him. Come to the trial. Bring evidence. Surely someone has seen something, has heard something. We can put the pieces together, and find the murderer, who- ever he might be."

The woman looked troubled, gazing away from Adrienne out toward where her husband was reaping the golden wheat. "My lady, all are afraid," she said finally, in a low tone. "It is a struggle between the priest, and the one we call—Lord Satan. He has a terrible temper. Who wants to be caught between them? And we are his tenants. It is best if we stay away."

"But if you all stay away, who will give evidence? Only the priest, and Granny Dille!" cried Adrienne pas- sionately. "For my sake—if you love me at all—come and help me! I love my husband. I would save him if it meant my life!"

The woman looked back at Adrienne, and her face softened. "We are afraid—but we will try to come, my lady," she promised simply. "I do not know if it will help—but I heard something. Perhaps—one might have

144

seen something," she added, very vaguely, but there was an eager light in her eyes.

"Oh, if anyone has seen something—if anyone will testify—beg them to come and help us!" pleaded Adrienne.

She went on to the next farm, which was that of Jennie Tyson's family. She found the father plowing in the fields, his face cold and hard. The woman sat on a stump in the yard, her hands in her apron, her face troubled, hurt. She spoke to them both, they gazed at her blankly.

She asked if the priest had been sent for. They shook their heads. "No. No, not the priest. He consorts with the witch, Granny Dille. We do not like him," they said.

"But come to the trial, my husband is accused of her murder! He did not do it. I want the guilty one found!" cried Adrienne. She felt more and more strongly about this, now she knew the priest had probably lied to her. He could have seen Jennie in town at the midwife's, but surely they would have told her if he had come.

They did not promise. She went on, gazing back quickly at the dumb suffering faces as they stared after her. They had been hurt, badly hurt. Their lovely Jennie, cut down and murdered in her budding womanhood.

She went on, and on, drinking tea with one family. She ate a sandwich at noon with another family, urging them to come to the trial. The groom was growing uneasy, growling that my lord would have his head if he didn't bring his lady back soon.

But she would go on, and she was firm. She went to the next farm, and the next. Some were silent with her, some were more talkative. The children came out, and listened, their faces curious, their eyes wide. She noticed one boy, about seven, who clung to his mother's skirts, in an unusual display of fear. The woman kept patting his head automatically, saying, "Now Billy, Billy, it's my lady here. Where are your manners?"

But he seemed to be dumb, and scared, staring up at Adrienne with fascinated blue eyes, as big and blue as her own. He was a tow-haired child, handsome and big for his age.

She said goodbye to his mother, and went on. At the village, she saw Granny Dille from a distance, but ignored her. She spoke to the baker, to the greengrocer, the apothecary, several women, urging them to come to the trial, to ask friends, to inquire if anyone had seen or heard anything that would be of help.

She went on and on. Some people were friendly, some reserved, some frightened, some cautious, some few were coldly hateful. No one promised to come to the trial.

She finally went home, exhausted, arriving at the castle about five in the afternoon. Vincent was waiting for her at the foot of the steps, anger in his eyes, concern in his face. He lifted her out of the carriage, cursed the groom soundly, and sent him away.

He carried Adrienne up the long flight of stairs, and set her down in the hallway. He lifted off her cloak, then put it around her again.

"You are chilled through. Do you deliberately set out to frighten me, Adrienne? Why did you not tell me you wished to ride? I would have accompanied you."

She clasped his hand with her small fingers, convulsively. "I do not mean to frighten you," she said, wearily. "I have been around to the farms and into the village. I have asked everyone I knew to come to the trial, to bring any small bit of evidence of the murders. Together, we can solve it, we must."

"You are mad, my love! No one has seen anything. No one has said a word!" He drew her into her pretty blue living room, and settled her on the couch.

"No one has said anything. That does not mean no one has seen! Vincent, it has happened again and again. Many of the folk here go out on the moors. Some run their dogs there, even the sheep sometimes nibble there. Someone, some time, must have seen something!" She sounded hysterical even to herself.

He soothed her, had tea brought, and held the cup for her, until she was more composed. She lay back, exhausted, and Vincent looked like he was ready to swear again, but with great restraint he kept his vocabulary at a polite level.

"You are not to go out again, Adrienne! If you cannot take care of yourself, you will force me to strong measures! I will not let you come to the trial, if you carry on so! In any event—" he paused, his face darkening. "It might be best if you do not come to it on Monday," he said, rather softly.

She understood him. If he were found guilty, and in his rage brought down fire, and then disappeared, she would best be away.

"No, Vincent, I shall come to your trial. You shall not keep me away! I shall be there, and you shall be vindicated," and she burst into tears of weariness and frustration.

"Now, be quiet, be quiet, love," he said, and soothed her, more troubled for her than for himself. Presently, he brought the baby to her, and encouraged her to feed it from her breasts. He sat and watched her feed the baby, and rock him, singing to him as he went off to a contented sleep. That helped to calm them both.

"Nothing can happen to us, Vincent," she said, as she laid small Vincent Jonathan in his basket. "I feel it strongly. Nothing can happen to us. All will be well."

"I shall manage, one way or another. I have laid my plans," he said, quietly. "You are not to worry or distress yourself, Adrienne. If I have to leave, I will take you and the babe with me. I shall not leave you."

"I know that, love," and she laid her hand in his big one. They sat and looked into the fire thoughtfully until supper time, and her thoughts were firmer now, and she planned also, quite different plans from those of her husband.

Monday came all too soon. Adrienne dressed carefully, in a warm blue wool dress, and her blue velvet cloak and bonnet. With her long blonde hair and her blue eyes and angelic face, her husband, fondly, said to her, "You look very like an angel, not like the wife of the devil they may soon know me to be!"

"You are not a devil any more, Vincent, I shall not admit it! You are more than half human, and you will be more so, as the years go on! Please, Vincent, do not be impulsive today. Stand quietly in the dock, and let evidence be brought." And she gazed up at him anxiously.

He had chosen to dress in the Caudill colors, his suit of ruby red velvet, and the black velvet cloak streaming out behind him. In his tension, his face was darkly saturnine, and his green eyes flashed with fire. She sighed, half because he was so handsome, half because he did look so devilish.

He wore huge red rubies on his hands, at his throat, and on his coat. They flashed and caught the sunlight, as they descended the steps to the waiting carriage. The groom looked even smarter today, she thought, in his red and black livery.

Vincent helped her into the carriage. He was very quiet

as they drove along the wide tree-lined path along the moors, out into the moors a brief way, then swung back into the path toward the village.

As they approached the village, they saw a far greater crowd of people than Adrienne had ever seen gathered.

"They have come for the spectacle, the priest and the devil, the priest versus the powers of evil!" Vincent laughed harshly.

Adrienne said, more firmly than she felt, "Right shall win, Vincent! You will see that today!"

"That will be something new. I have not seen it before," he laughed again. She noticed that people on the street shrank back from the carriage as they drove along, Vincent with his head back laughing. They stared up at him with fascinated eyes.

She smiled at some as they went, and a few smiled back timidly. She knew them now, the grocer's wife, the innkeeper's lady, the maids at the inn, the baker and his family, the grooms from the livery stable, many of the people of the town. And the tenants were there, in their Sunday clothes.

She saw many of them, the Tysons, Kevin and Lauranne Prestwick and their child Giselle fairylike in her blonde beauty. She saw Mrs. Dawes and her husband and Billy, sturdy in a blue suit, his blonde head back, his blue eyes staring up at her. She saw others, the tenant whose grass had "gone bad," and his son who had diagnosed the trouble accurately. The boy waved at them, and even grinned at Vincent shyly. Vincent, surprised, waved back at him.

The sheriff came out to speak to them as the carriage pulled up at the town hall. "You came," he said, as though surprised. He stood awkwardly as Vincent helped Adrienne down, and turned to escort them into the hall. "You, sir, you have to go to the dock to be charged," he said, unhappily, as they entered.

"Right," said Vincent curtly. "Let me escort my wife to a seat. She has been ill."

"Oh, yes, sir, yes, sir, right at the front here," and the sheriff hurriedly took them forward. The hall was filling rapidly. Adrienne saw the priest sitting at a table with several lawyers at the front of the room. He turned to glare at them as they came.

His face was white today, white and long and startling in its lines. His hair was wild and wind-tossed. She wondered if he had been walking on the moors. Granny Dille was there, sitting across the room on a front bench, leaning on her cane, her eyes sly and eagerly alert.

All too soon the trial began. The judge came in, and the charges were intoned. The long list of charges, the names of the girls murdered, and "their bodies dismembered" on the moors. As she turned about slightly, she could see the young faces of the children alert and fascinated. The adults seemed apprehensive, their eyes flickering, their heads turning from priest to Vincent standing in the dock, his red coat and his black cloak setting him off against the dark wood of the box.

Vincent's hands were clasped loosely on the edge of the box. His green eyes glittered as the charges were read. She saw the red in the green flecking their depths. She saw how the people looked at Vincent's hands, as the charges were speaking of the hands of the murderer and how they had ripped at the bodies of the young girls.

Silence when the charges had been made. Then evidence was requested. The priest was up at once, and spoke at length. The man was a devil, he said, and went raving on about black masses, Vincent's father, strange occurrences in the castle when all the servants were changed.

The judge listened with some patience, until too long a time had gone. Then he rapped sharply with his gavel. "These have nothing to do with the murders, Reverend Father," he said sharply. "I warn you to give evidence on the charges at hand. Have you seen this man on the moors at the time of the murders?"

"No, I have not seen him there, but know the man for a devil, and he is to be exposed. Evil must be exposed and wiped clean!" cried the priest, his face flushing, his black eyes glittering. He twisted about, until his hands looked like long thin scarecrow hands, and his black cloak was flying.

"Then if you have no evidence to give, you will be seated!" said the judge sternly. He looked about the courtroom. "Has anyone else evidence to give!"

Granny Dille piped up, "I saw them, I saw them on the moors, the pretty ones, all the pretty ones, raped and torn and with knives in their pretty stomachs!"

A chill went down Adrienne's spine, as the old woman came to stand in front of the box. Vincent stared down at her, frowning, from his height.

"I saw the murders," she cried again, and a shudder went through the room. "I saw them! I saw the devil here committing murders! I saw things, I have seen them for a thousand years! I have seen the devils in hell, committing their shameful acts! I have seen battles of the devils and angels—"

The judge sighed deeply. "Someone get the woman to sit down," he said wearily. "I am asking for true evidence on this case, not the ravings of a woman—such as this."

Adrienne leaned back with a sigh of relief, her spine feeling like a wet flower stem.

"Can anyone give true evidence?" asked the judge again. "Let him speak. Has anyone seen anything?"

The farmer who had rescued Jennie Tyson finally stood up, his face red, worried, embarrased. "I seen some things, Your Honor," he said shyly.

"Come forward and be sworn."

He came forward, stumbling a little. Adrienne again was conscious that the boy, Billy Dawes, was staring at her with his big blue eyes. She smiled at him. Maybe one day her small Vincent Jonathan would be such a big sturdy boy as this, she thought fondly. The boy kept staring at her, gravely, and finally timidly smiled back, a little jerk of his lips. Then he stared down again, and cringed back against his mother.

The farmer was telling his story, with a monotone which told of how often he had gone over and over this very story. "So I saw this black figure on the moors. It was in a black cloak, it was."

"What did the cloak look like?" asked the judge. "Like the one my lord here is wearing?"

"Yes, sir, or the priest. Like any other black cloak," said the farmer, uneasily, then flushed. "I mean—it was just a man in a black cloak. Couldn't make out his face no how. He seemed to be beckoning to me, and pointing down at something on the moors. Then he disappeared."

"Disappeared? How did he disappear?" asked the judge sharply.

"I don't know, sir. I didn't want to come no closer. I was skeered. Then he just wasn't there. I whipped up me horse, and druv close. Then I seen it was a girl there, all naked and bloody. Took me a spell to see it was Jennie Tyson. I wanted to run away, but then she moaned, and I seen she was alive and moving. So I lifted her up and covered her with my coat, and took her into town."

150

The judge questioned him again and again, but his story was unchanged. He had seen a figure in a black cloak, motioning him closer. He had rescued Jennie, and she had told him the attacker had hurt her, that was all.

The farmer went back to his seat. There was an awkward silence. All were staring at Vincent, at his hands, at his face, his broad shoulders, his eyes. Vincent stared back at them defiantly, his scowl deepening, the red flecks flashing in his green eyes.

Adrienne clasped her hands tightly, and prayed desperately. Let someone come forward and speak, she prayed. Let someone help. If only someone knew something, let them speak, let them help. Oh, God, she prayed. Help my Vincent. I want him to become good and fine as he is capable of becoming. If he is found guilty, he will go wild, and expose himself as a devil, and all will be lost. There will be no turning back. Oh, God, help us!

In the silence of the courtroom, a small voice sounded, the voice of a child.

"I seen it," said the voice.

Adrienne stiffened, turned, to see Billy Dawes coming forward slowly, pulling his startled mother with him.

"I seen it," he said again, staring toward the judge steadily. He came up even with Adrienne, then seemed to lose his courage. He was clinging to his mother's hand, and to her apron with the other hand. His face was so white the freckles stood out like red spots.

"Who are you?" asked the judge gently. He was from another town.

"Billy—Dawes, please."

"Billy, what did you see?"

The boy wet his lips. He did not look away from the judge. Some inner force seemed to be driving him. "I was out—on the moors—in the summer. My dog, he got away. I went for him. Out on the moors."

"When was this, Billy? In August?"

He seemed to think. "No, it was July," he said. "I followed my dog on the moors."

"What happened?"

The silence in the courtroom was intense. Everyone was leaning forward, staring at the child, peering from Vincent's dark face to the priest to the judge.

"I heard my dog barking. I went to get him. It was getting dark. I heard him crying. I thought an animal done got him. I went up near. I saw a man bending over my

151

dog. He slashed down with a knife. Like this." And Billy let go his mother's apron long enough to slash his hand up and down fiercely. "I hid behind a rock. I was scared. I saw the blood coming, and my dog stopped crying, and I knowed he was dead."

"The man killed your dog, yes, Billy. That was what you saw," said the judge.

A small dissatisfied sigh went up from the crowd.

"Yes, and I waited," said Billy. "The man, he was waiting. Then I saw Flora."

The crowd stiffened again. Adrienne grasped her hands so tightly together, that they hurt.

"Flora. Flora Moberly," asked the judge, very softly. His eyes were shining as he listened.

"Yes, sir. Flora. She was walking along the moors. The man, he hid. I wanted to scream at Flora, but I was scared. I waited, and I saw him jump out. She run, but he cotched her. He knocked her down, and he lied down on her. Hard, and his hands on her throat. He let her loose once, and she was saying my God my God oh let me go oh my God my God—" The small innocent voice repeated the words as though they were on his school slate.

The judge let him talk. The words poured out.

"And then—and then—the man—he got up, and he took a knife. And Flora screamed, she screamed my God don't don't don't—and he slashed down—like he done to my dog—and he cut her throat from one ear around to the other ear, and the blood it pushed up from her and got all over the man's hands and over his knife. And he laughed," said the child, his eyes wide with the wonder of it. "The man, he laughed. And he slashed again—and again. She was naked. He slashed all down herself, down to her feet. All over. Until she was all blood."

Adrienne was panting, her mouth open, not wanting to make a sound. Sick, sick, but needing to hear. She was staring at the child, as were all the others.

"Who was the man, Billy? Is he here in the courtroom?" asked the judge, very slowly, his face flushed.

The tow head moved up and down. He shrank back against his mother's skirt, and hid his face for a moment.

"The man is here in the courtroom, Billy? Will you point to the man you saw, the man—who slashed your dog—and slashed Flora—point to him?"

The judge had a commanding calm voice. Billy moved, and the small arm came up. The finger pointed out, a grimy finger, a sturdy small finger, pointing steadily, and he was looking where he pointed, his finger pointed.

And they all looked where he pointed—

At the priest!

"No—no—he lies! The boy lies! He never saw me! No one was there!" The priest had jumped up, his white face had turned red and furious. His black eyes glittered insanely. "He never saw me. I was performing the black mass! It was necessary!"

"You did the deed?" asked the judge gravely.

"I did it! It was necessary! I had to know how the black mass was done. One must know the ways of the devil before one can defeat him! And she had sinned! All those girls had sinned! They came to me in confession, and told how they stroked themselves! They told me their sinful ways, and I longed to cleanse them! Yes, I had to cleanse them—with blood! Wipe out their sins with blood!"

The small accusing finger of the boy still pointed steadily as the priest raved. Now Adrienne could smell the sulphur smell strongly in the room—and it was from the priest. It was stifling, sickening in that room.

"I had to do it!" raved the priest, the blood foaming on his wide lips. He waved his arms wildly, the black cloak flapping behind him. "I had to do it! I had to wipe them clean of their sins! And I had to know the black mass! I had sacrificed animals, but they are not human!"

The room was very hushed.

Even Vincent was staring down at the priest in surprise, thought Adrienne, sparing a glance at her husband. He seemed as shocked as they all were.

"They were not human! I had to have a human sacrifice for my altar to Satan! He demands human sacrifice—human—human—blood on the moors—human blood—blood on the moors—" screamed the priest, and collapsed.

They all rose, as one, and stared down at him. He moaned, twisted, blood trickling from his mouth. Then he lay still, very still.

Finally the sheriff went over to him, knelt down awkwardly in his heavy uniform, and touched his pulse, touched his head.

"Dead," he said.

The judge rose, imposing in his robes and white wig. "The prisoner is released, cleared of the charges placed against him. The priest will be written on the records as the guilty one, damned by his own confession," said the judge, and walked from the room.

In the babble of talk that went up, Adrienne found herself swaying. Vincent was soon beside her, holding her close to him. "My darling, my darling, your faith—" he whispered. "It has shamed—the devil!"

And he dared to laugh down at her. She laughed back, rather feebly, clinging to him.

The secret that Vincent was really a devil was safe—for now.

CHAPTER 18

Vincent came in from the gardens, bringing a bouquet of late roses and the fresh scents of the outdoors with him. He smiled down at Adrienne in her blue chair, with the baby in her lap, and put the flowers in her hand.

"The babe grows daily," he said, with great satisfaction, and dropped a kiss on the soft down of its head. The baby stirred, held out its arms demandingly. Vincent lifted him up, held him high above his head, then lowered him to rest against his shoulder. He sat down in a big chair near Adrienne. He holds the baby so carefully, she thought. He really adored the small child.

"He really smiled at me today," said Adrienne, and got up to ring for a vase for the flowers. When it was brought, she arranged the pretty pink and white roses in the blue slim vase, and set the vase near her on one of the small tables. Then she sat down on the couch, and picked up one of the toys Roderick Stanton had left on his latest visit. It was a small gold box enameled on four sides, with lapis lazuli, diamonds and amethysts decorating it in elaborate symbolic designs. "This box is so odd, Vincent. Do you know what these things mean?"

When he did not answer, she looked up at him. He was staring at her thoughtfully, his face serious.

"Do you, Vincent? Do they mean something special?"

He nodded. "Yes, they do, my dear. Father and I were

154

discussing matters when he was here last. He wants you to attend a black mass, come to know some matters you should understand. I said I would speak to you about it."

She felt the sudden familiar sinking of her spirits. Vincent had begun to urge her more and more often to attend the black mass with him, to learn the Satanic rites.

"I cannot, Vincent," she said, as steadily as possible. She set down the box as though it would burn her fingers. It was so pretty—and so dangerous.

"You love knowledge. How can you refuse to learn such important secrets? Most persons would give their very souls to grasp the secrets of the universe which we offer to you freely," said Vincent. His jade green eyes were narrowed.

"I prefer to trust in God and his goodness to us," she said. "He has treated us well, Vincent, far better than we deserve. He has saved you, for I prayed heartily for your safety."

He frowned quickly as she said the word "God," but he did not curse, as he used to do. "I would not have been harmed," he said, roughly. "I have my own powers! They would not have held me longer than a moment, had I chosen!"

"One thing still puzzles me," she said, thankful for the slight change of subject. "Who was the figure in the black cloak on the moors, the one who beckoned to the farmer?"

"Oh—that. I have the report from Satan. He had the priest followed by a devil, who observed all. It was the devil who frightened the priest from the dying body of Jennie Tyson, and beckoned to the farmer to come and get her. He then reported to Satan that the priest was doing all the murders. We should have had the report before the trial. I cursed them for their slowness, I can assure you!"

She shivered a little, staring into the fire in the huge fireplace. Every now and then, she had a glimpse into this other mysterious world, and it made reality itself seem strange and unfamiliar. Dark deeds and evil were all through the world, and devils roamed it at will. She must be constantly on her guard, she thought.

He seemed to read her mind, and indeed she thought he could.

"Adrienne, give in! I wish this! You can do much good with your new powers! Learn of me, I will teach you slowly and gently about the secrets of the universe! You shall learn to travel where you choose—though I will not let you travel alone, my darling! I am jealous of you, and will go with you always!" And he laughed, and the baby laughed with him.

Adrienne looked over at them fondly, the large strong man, so dark and handsome and devilish, the baby, so little and fragile and sweet. "You are my lives, my loves," she said simply. "Without you, I would die. I have no wish to go anywhere alone, or to leave you. I have not the strength your mother has, to refuse to see you again. But indeed, Vincent, I will not participate in your Satanic rites. I refuse this. It is evil, and the power you use is evil. It is not meant for man, for any human being, to have so much power and wealth."

"I have it," he said, and shrugged. "I have it, and you could have it. Is it wrong that I wish to share my powers with you? The babe will have need of your guidance when his time comes to learn this also." And he stroked his large hand tenderly over the small downy head.

"Oh—no, Vincent, no," she cried. "I do not want him to be trained in this!"

He looked his surprise and reproof. "He is my son. He is part devil, as I am," he said, coldly. "He will learn. He has the powers already, I have observed him. Watch him now. Babe, bring up the fire!"

As she caught her breath in dismay, the tiny uncertain fist waved, and at once the fire in the fireplace leaped up in a roar, consuming the huge log there. The baby laughed in delight.

"No—no—no—" moaned Adrienne, in distress. She sprang up, and reached out imploringly for the baby. Vincent gave him into her arms at once.

"Do not distress yourself unduly," he said, still sternly. "The babe has powers. He will learn to train them. Without training, he will not use them wisely. But leave him to me. Now, we will have a black mass tonight. I want you to come, Adrienne!"

She shook her head dumbly, bent her head over the baby in her arms, and slow painful tears filled her eyes. Vincent softened at once, and put his arms about them both.

"There now, don't weep. I didn't mean to make you weep. There, love, dry your eyes. I cannot bear for you to cry."

Tenderly he dried her eyes with his handkerchief of fine lawn, teased her to make her smile, and finally left her with the babe, to make preparations for the mass that night, he said.

She sat down in front of the fire again, drawing the child close to her for comfort. He was sucking his fist, cuddling down against her. He seemed so little and helpless. Could he actually practice powers, or had Vincent teased her, and done the fire trick himself?

She gazed at the fire for a long time. Then she noticed the baby was looking toward the fire also, his blue eyes turning to green now.

He would have green eyes eventually, like Vincent's, she thought.

"Vincent Jonathan," she said softly. "Turn up the fire."

Obediently he stretched out his small wavering fist, and the fire leaped up and consumed another large log which Vincent had placed on it.

"Oh, dear God," she whispered.

The baby quivered and seemed to shiver, wincing from the word.

She closed her eyes. The baby was truly part devil, small as he was. Vincent was right about that also. Her child was part devil.

She sat there for a long time, thinking, agonizing. What could she do? She had thought to change Vincent, to keep her baby innocent of evil. Had she failed completely?

Vincent had seemed to change the past few weeks and months. He was softened by love and trust, no longer so violent of temper, no longer hard and unfeeling. The tenants had come to trust him somewhat. She could see the change in them when she and Vincent went to see them.

The farmers spoke to him more freely, asked his advice, listened to him. When he spoke of how to treat a sick horse, his advice was followed to the letter. When he advised on a farm, they did what he said. When a housewife told of an illness, he recommended and even brought herbs to her.

"He knows a mighty peck of stuff," said one woman admiringly. "He knows much more than Granny Dille, and he knows *right*, not like that one."

Granny Dille was a pathetic soul these days. Evidently the priest had been her master, not the other way around. She had lost all her reputation for witchcraft, and no one listened to her or bought her remedies. The last Adrienne had heard, the old woman had packed up on a donkey, and left the village for parts unknown, where she evidently hoped to frighten someone into paying her way in life.

The evil seemed to have left the village, with the death of the priest and the departure of its witch. Now the word was that the new priest was coming, a young earnest man who did much good in his work. The parishioners were hopefully waiting and praying for his arrival.

"If only," murmured Adrienne to herself, "if only I could have cleansed Vincent's soul for him, if only I could have taken his evil on myself and changed him. If only——"

But ifs did no good, she thought. She must work constantly to change him. She must not give in to his pleadings, his orders, his charm, and participate in the black mass. Lady Guinevere had advised her again and again against this. It would be fatal for her, she told Adrienne. The mind was gripped and enchanted, she would no longer be mistress of her will.

Love will change him, she thought. Love must change him. She would love and trust him, and slowly, slowly, he would continue to change and put off his old bad ways. Maybe someday he would give up the black mass and Satanic rites, also, though she could not be at all sure of that. He seemed to adore them, to find strength and fresh powers in the rites.

He was restless also. The last time Roderick had come, the father had almost persuaded his son to come with him on a trip, an adventure down a strange river called the Amazon. Great treasures and beauties were to be seen, said Roderick, and cordially invited Adrienne to come also.

She had said she would not leave her baby, and she would not. But Vincent had been sorely tempted, she had seen.

One day Vincent might give in to the temptation and leave them for a time. But she resolved to keep on loving and trusting him. She and baby together would draw them back to them, with the need they had for him.

Love would cure all.

Vincent came into the room, softly. "Are you asleep, you are both so quiet."

He sat down beside her. "Not asleep, love, only dreaming," she said, and put her head down contentedly on his shoulder.

"I have finally found something to give little Billy Dawes," said Vincent.

She half-sat up. He pushed her head back to his shoulder.

"We must not give him rich gifts," she said, urgently, as she had before. "It would be suspect then, that we had bribed him to give evidence."

"Hush now, we have spoken of this before. No one could find this amiss. The bitch has had five fine pups. He shall have his choice of them, one to replace his dog. Do you mind that dreadfully?" asked Vincent, and chuckled.

"Oh, no, that will be fine. Is the bitch all right?"

"Yes, fine."

"Oh, Billy will like that. We shall have him come and choose soon," she said happily. She thought, in the old days, Vincent would never have thought of such a considerate gift. He would not have thought of the love of a boy for his dog, that the gift would be more welcome to a seven-year-old boy than the finest diamond in the world.

"Yes, you have changed me," said Vincent, softly into her ear. He had read her mind again, with his usual shrewdness. "But do not change me too much. I shall be neither man nor devil!"

"Oh, you are very much—man—" she whispered, and turned up her face for his kisses. He gathered her up, being careful of the babe, and pressed his lips passionately to her cheeks and then her mouth. His lips opened on hers, and the fire leaped hotly between them.

She gasped a little at the passion in him, and surrendered herself gladly to it. This passion she knew and comprehended, though he could still amaze her with it.

When he held her in bed, and lay on her, and made her very mind swim with his love, and her body tremble and shake, and her limbs tingle and quiver, she did not know if he had the power of man or devil or both— All she knew was that she loved and adored him so much her small body seemed unable to contain it all.

She loved him—man or devil—all Vincent. All the conqueror who had won her heart and mind and soul.